His lips were teasing and tantalizing

It had been so long since a man had held her, and the pressure of the hard body against hers, the eager probing of his mouth, was driving her slightly crazy. His mouth moved sideways, kissing a heated path, to nibble seductively beneath her ear.

"Nicki!" He buried his face in the gleaming tumble of her hair. "Why you?" he murmured vaguely.

Crystals of awareness exploded in Nicole's head. Drew was no lover. He was a—a hater of her. Or at least of the type of girl he believed her to be. A tempting female body was the sum total of what she represented. Florida fever must exist, for he seemed to have forgotten that at heart he despised her. Her brain must be fevered, too, for why else was she succumbing so readily to his caresses?

ELIZABETH OLDFIELD
is also the author of these

Harlequin Presents

604—DREAM HERO
608—SECOND TIME AROUND

These books may be available at your local bookseller.

For a free catalog listing all titles currently available,
send your name and address to:

HARLEQUIN READER SERVICE
1440 South Priest Drive, Tempe, AZ 85281
Canadian address: Stratford, Ontario N5A 6W2

ELIZABETH OLDFIELD

florida fever

Harlequin Books

TORONTO • NEW YORK • LONDON
AMSTERDAM • PARIS • SYDNEY • HAMBURG
STOCKHOLM • ATHENS • TOKYO • MILAN

Harlequin Presents first edition October 1983
ISBN 0-373-10637-8

Original hardcover edition published in 1983
by Mills & Boon Limited

CHAPTER ONE

BLUE-GREY smoke spiralled as Drew Benedict took a final impatient drag at the slim panatella. 'Don't waste time, start negotiations immediately. Screw them into the ground if you can,' he ordered, jabbing the remains of the cigar into oblivion. 'Keep me informed of developments. *Ciao*.'

He jettisoned the phone, the corner of his mouth lifting in apology to a young man who was lounging, arms folded, beside the window wall.

'Sorry, Brian, ever since I crawled in through the door this morning it's been all systems go.' He twisted to peel away a navy pin-striped jacket, haphazardly thrusting it over the back of his chair. 'Where were we?' he demanded, as he unhooked embossed silver cufflinks and began rolling up the sleeves of a snow-white shirt to expose muscled forearms.

'Interviews for the Key Benedict post,' his brother prompted.

Beneath the dark bristly moustache, Drew's mouth quirked into amusement. 'Ah yes! Have you found me a luscious blue-blooded nymph with perfect French and an I.Q. of two hundred and ten?'

There was a disgusted snort. 'You're asking the impossible and you know it!'

'I can live in hope.'

Automatically he reached again for the gold-edged packet and the young man deserted his bird's eye view of the city streets to stride forward.

'You're smoking too much.'

'Quit acting as my conscience!' The retort contained a whiplash of temper, but Drew's fingers stilled and he flipped the packet aside. 'I took enough flak last Sunday. What everyone forgets is that being continually on the move is no joke. Hell! I spend my life flying from one godforsaken airport to the next, I must relax somehow."

Brian registered the defiance which had tightened his brother's jaw. 'Why don't you take a holiday? I can't remember the last time you broke loose.'

Easing himself into the swivel chair, Drew stretched, the fine silk moulding across his chest. 'I will—some time,' he agreed vaguely.

'I mean it. If you don't, you're going to crack up.'

'Oh, you sound more like Mum every day! Next thing you'll be complaining that my hair's too long and that I should gain weight. I swear that woman wouldn't be satisfied if I resembled the Michelin Man.' Drew ground the base of his palms into his eyes and rubbed furiously. 'And if you dare to hint that it's high time I was married again, I shall sling you out of the window, twenty stories up or not, so lay off!'

'Once bitten, twice shy,' Brian chanted glibly.

'Poppycock! I haven't met the right woman, that's all.'

'Ha ha.'

'And what does that mean?' Drew demanded, his voice edged.

'It means you keep well away from anyone who's half decent.' Brian pulled down the corners of his mouth. 'Okay, so the girls you date are fine as short-term playmates, but you must admit not one has been the type you would want to spend the rest of your life with. Seems to me you're frightened to make a commitment.'

Drew gave a loud bark of derision. 'One thing is clear, I don't need to waste money on a psychiatrist while my family is available! Many thanks for the homespun analysis, but as usual you're way off centre.' He lifted his long legs to rest his feet on the corner of the over-sized teak desk. 'Shall we get back to business?'

'You know I'm right.' Doggedly Brian refused to abandon the subject. 'The fact that you've never taken a girl along to the Sunday lunches proves it.'

'Life would be a darn sight simpler if I avoided the Sunday lunches, period.' Drew tugged roughly at the knot of his maroon tie. 'Then I'd escape the not-so-sly digs and innuendoes. How come everyone—but everyone—wants to run my life for me?'

Brian's hazel eyes crinkled at the corners. 'Stop complaining—a bit of family concern can't hurt. Besides, you know you come on Sundays whenever you can. Mum's one heck of a good cook.'

Drew conceded the point. 'But if she mentions Karen and those kids of hers one more time——' he threatened ominously.

'She won't. I realised you were about to blow your top last week, so I had a discreet word. The message has gone home.'

'I damn well hope so,' he growled, then, at the buzz of the intercom, leant forward to lift a switch. 'Yes, Jenny?'

'Have you had a chance to sign the mail, Mr Benedict?' his secretary asked.

Swinging his legs from the desk, Drew straightened briskly, reaching for the folder. 'I'm sorry. The phone has never stopped ringing and I've been trying to catch up on Brian's side of the business.' He glanced at the black-faced watch on his wrist. 'Look, it's almost six. If you want to leave I'll sign the letters and put them into the post myself.'

'No, no, I don't mind waiting,' Jenny assured him hastily, and they could hear her smile.

'I'll get busy right now,' he promised.

'That girl would dance barefoot on broken glass for you—they all would,' Brian smiled, as Drew turned to root out a fountain-pen from his jacket. 'If only I'd been blessed with baby-blue eyes and three-inch lashes!'

Coarse words greeted his comment, but he gave an unrepentant laugh, ambling back across the thick carpet to watch the stop-start samba of the traffic through the London streets. It was late May, a mild sunny evening, perfect for driving out to some country pub and eating chicken-in-a-basket, washed down with pints of lager. He smiled ruefully. With Drew around there was no chance of a carefree evening. Past experience proved they were destined to remain office-bound until nightfall, as his brother familiarised himself with what had been happening in the various branches of the Benedict empire during his absence abroad.

Brian folded his arms, waiting again as Drew worked through the letters. Even a stranger would have known the two men were related, for all four Benedict sons were tall and broad-shouldered, with gipsy-dark hair, but only Drew, second in line, had compelling blue eyes and thick black lashes—a combination which had been proving irresistible to women for the past twenty years.

Minutes later Jenny scurried in to collect the mail, dimpling prettily at her employer's gratitude for her forbearance.

'Go ahead,' Drew commanded when the office was quiet again. 'How are the Key Benedict interviews progressing?'

'I've seen six girls so far, and one seems possible, though her French is a little shaky.'

Drew shook his head, a few strands of black hair tumbling carelessly across his brow. 'She won't do. I've told you before that a percentage of our clients are French-Canadians, so fluent French is vital.'

'Fluent French, immaculate education, pleasant manner and *style*!' the younger man grumbled, striding back to perch on the edge of the desk.

'Especially style.' The confirmation was deadly serious. 'The girl will be handling wealthy clients. They must feel she's an equal, that her opinions matter, that they can rely on her. But she must have the common touch, I don't want her too high and mighty.'

'Or else she might put *you* in your place!'

The thrust provoked a lurching grin. 'She could try.'

'I suppose you would like thirty-six—twenty-four—thirty-six as well?' Brian added facetiously.

'I'm not too fussy on that,' Drew chuckled. 'I'd settle for a thirty-eight—up top, naturally.'

His brother gave a sarcastic guffaw.

'Don't despair,' Drew continued. 'You're seeing a further six tomorrow, aren't you?'

'Seven. Out of the blue I received a letter from some girl who has stayed in several of our properties. She wrote to ask if there were any vacancies abroad for holiday guides or receptionists. She also speaks good French, or so she says.' He shrugged. 'I decided to interview her as well.'

'What's her name?'

'Nicole Smith.'

'Huh, Smith doesn't sound too promising. She's probably a shop girl who spent a fortnight at one of our small apartments on the Costa Brava.'

'Snob!' Brian chided.

'I'm not, but the Key Benedict complex is light years away from package holidays in Spain. It's a multi-million-dollar investment providing luxury for the super-tax bracket. I need a stylish lady for a stylish job!'

His brother gave way to the exasperation simmering below the surface. 'Come and look over the applicants yourself, if you're so damn fussy, and then you'll see what I'm up against. I've sifted through nearly a hundred replies and, believe me, the ones I'm interviewing are the cream.'

'I'm sure they are,' Drew agreed. 'But you know how close Key Benedict is to my heart. I want everything to be right. It's all gone so well, so far. It would be a shame to louse it up by a wrong appointment. It's our biggest development yet. The first condominiums were snapped up and already we're processing enquiries for the second phase. The hotel is booked for months ahead and now the villas are the finishing touch.' His eyes shone with pride. 'They're superb.'

'At almost a million dollars each, they should be!'

'Ten architect-designed homes, situated amongst lush tropical greenery on a private island in Florida,' Drew continued, leaning back in his chair. 'Overlooking a secluded bay with its own marina. What more could you want?' He lifted a questioning hand.

'Miss Super-de-luxe to sell them!' Brian grumbled.

Peering at herself in the mirror, Nicole Smith stretched her grey-green eyes extra-wide and delicately finger-tipped in a contact lens.

'Ouch!' she grimaced, and plucked it right out again.

It had hurt. Blinking rapidly, she studied the tiny transparent disc, searching for a clue to her discomfort. Oh no! there was a tiny jag on one side. Panic stirred. how had that happened? And why now? Her stomach curdled as she realised the implications. Her eye could not tolerate a torn lens, it would be sheer agony, yet she had no replacement so the only alternative was to wear her spectacles. But they made her feel so dowdy! And this morning, in less than an hour, she was due to attend an interview, an interview for a job which could mean an end to all her problems—a job it was vital she land.

If she wore her spectacles she was destined to be an also-ran. It was quite true, men did not make passes at girls who wore glasses—well, not too often—and the same went for interviews. Her fine gold-rimmed spectacles might bear the logo of an exclusive Parisian fashion house and have cost the earth, but they were still spectacles, and at twenty-four Nicole was realistic enough to know looks *did* count, no matter what anyone said. She pouted. She was damned if she would reduce her chances, when she needed all the ammunition she could muster. Pushing the shiny russet-brown hair from her brow, she decided there was no alternative but to attempt to steer her way through the interview half-blind. In all modesty she knew her wide-set eyes were two of her greatest assets. Roberto had waxed lyrical over them, but that was Roberto's style. Even Charlie, who had been far more pragmatic, had once said they reminded him of twin sea-pools, deep and mysterious. Charlie, dear Charlie . . .

Not today, Nicole, she told herself firmly. There was no time for reminiscences, no 'if only', no 'what might have been'. It had taken months to grow new skin across her emotional wounds, and now was not the time for picking at it. She jammed the spectacles on to her short straight nose as a temporary measure and continued to dress.

Hmm, not bad, she decided at last, eyeing herself critically in the pockmarked mirror. She posed for an invisible photographer, fingers skimming one sleek hip, an elegant ankle projected at precisely the correct stance to show off the shape of her calf. Inspecting her face, she admitted that her jaw was a little too wide, her mouth a touch too generous, for classical beauty, but she had chic, and that was what mattered. Her mother had always maintained Frenchwomen were born with chic, and that Nicole's sense of style had been inherited along with her portion of Gallic blood.

She smoothed down the thick russet hair. To some it would seem sheer extravagance to spend more than twenty pounds on a haircut, especially when her finances were precarious, to say the least. But she regarded the skills of the top London stylist as a worthwhile investment. You got what you paid for, and Nicole smiled at her mirror image, satisfied with the whispered fringe, brushed to one side, the heavy fall of hair cut blunt at her shoulders. Mademoiselle Pontier would be proud of her. In the pastel pink linen suit,

with handmade court shoes and matching clutch bag,
her appearance faithfully followed the rules of good
grooming meted out at the Swiss school.

'A lady uses cosmetics discreetly, *mes enfants*,'
Mademoiselle Pontier had insisted. 'And never forget,
good food and good health equal good looks.'

Nicole gave a tiny snort. What did Mademoiselle
know? For months now she had been existing on junk
food with no apparent ill effect, for her hair still
bounced with vitality and her complexion remained
peach-smooth. But for how long? Perhaps she was
coasting along on a residue of the good life and,
one morning, would awaken to find herself as down-
at-heel and lacklustre as her surroundings? She
swept an uneasy look around the tiny room. The
carpet was threadbare, the few pieces of furniture
old and scratched, and previous occupants had spent
many happy hours thumbnailing off slivers of wallpaper.

'Miss Smith!'

A yodel came from below, and Nicole shook away
her thoughts to poke her head, spectacles and all, out of
the door.

'Telephone for you.' Her landlady was at the foot of
the stairs and when she lifted her brows in query, the
woman manoeuvred a cigarette to one corner of her
mouth and mumbled, 'It's a Mrs Foster.'

High heels clattering on the bare wooden staircase,
Nicole hurtled down.

'Good morning, my dear, Brenda Foster speaking,' a
voice said, and her spine stiffened with suspicion. Mrs
Foster's tone was over-warm and cloying. 'My husband
and I wondered if you could come round this evening.
There's a matter we would like to discuss. It's—er—it's
about our arrangement.'

'Do you want to leave Honeysuckle Haven?' Nicole
probed, standing to attention.

There was a shrill of laughter. 'Good heavens, no! It's not that at all.'

She sagged with silent relief. 'I'll try to be with you by eight.' For a moment she stood, biting her lip, then she rang off.

'You do look classy this morning,' a voice commented, and Nicole whirled round. Her landlady was leaning against the banister, royal-blue plastic hair rollers transforming her into some kind of monster from outer space. 'I was telling my Bert what beautiful outfits you wear. Pale colours look so expensive.'

'They're expensive to maintain,' Nicole sighed. 'I never considered dry-cleaning bills when I bought my clothes, and now I wish I'd been more practical.' She glanced down at the pale pristine suit. 'If I get just one dirty mark on this, it's ruined.'

'No doubt a young lady like you is very particular,' the woman remarked, puffing at her cigarette.

'Not as particular as I used to be,' Nicole answered, without thinking. 'My standards have been forced to fall. I never used to live like this.'

When a vexed shadow darkened the woman's face, Nicole realised what she had said and her cheeks began to redden. Oh, heavens, she had done it again! She seemed to be continually offending people with her innocent references to her former affluence, when that was her last intention.

'Um—I'd better go,' she said, gasping when she read the time on her watch. 'Would you excuse me, please?'

'Carry on,' the woman sniffed. The flimsy door slammed shut behind Nicole and she never heard the end of the sentence. 'It will do a madam like you good to realise what life is like for the other half!'

Nicole perched on the edge of the seat as the taxi wheedled its way through the West End traffic. There were five minutes in which to reach the Benedict offices, for what had been intended to be a leisurely preparation for the interview had developed into a mad dash, thanks to the torn contact lens and Mrs Foster's worrying phone call. Also she had planned to take the Underground, and here she was, wasting money on a taxi! Nicole gulped in a deep breath to summon up her usual poise, then grinned as the Benedict office tower came into view. Quickly she whipped the glasses from her nose. If only she had been in one of the sunny lands where she had spent much of her life, then she would have been content to wear her spectacles, for they had light-sensitive lenses which changed from clear to dark and back again; and she could have pretended they were merely sun-specs. But here, in London on a cloudy May morning—no, the idea was impossible. From now on her view of things would be on the blurry side, but she would manage!

Thrusting the correct fare into the driver's hand, she jumped from the taxi. The man's surly thanks told her he had expected a tip, but she hardened her heart. Although he would never believe it, her need was greater than his! As he departed with a noisy revving of the engine and a scornful backward glance, Nicole gazed up at the skyscraper and set her mouth into a line of determination. White clouds were scudding across the sky, and as she started over the broad pavement the wind tossed a handful of hair into her face. With a tiny moue of exasperation, she pushed it aside. Bending her head for a last-minute check on her appearance, one of Mademoiselle's golden rules, Nicole strode forward. Once more the wind whipped strands of lustrous brown hair over her eyes and, plucking at it, she discovered her path was obstructed.

'Sorry,' she said to a tall masculine figure in a grey suit. She stepped left. The man stepped left.

'So sorry,' Nicole repeated, side-stepping right.

The man moved right, too. Without looking up, she

automatically lifted a hand to guide her way past, but the broad chest was solid.

'Excuse me,' she said with a bite of determination.

She stepped left again. He stepped left. Realising what his game was, she glared wildly through the lace of tumbled hair. Just her luck to encounter some wolf intent on a pick-up when she had only seconds to spare! She flashed him a furious look and intent on escape, did not notice that his blue eyes were roving approvingly over her.

'I would like to pass,' she snapped in arctic tones, peering beyond his shoulder at the blurry haven of the office building. She strode right. He strode right.

'Poppet, we could take this act to Broadway, we synchronise so well,' a deep voice chuckled.

Nicole saw red. Poppet, indeed! She was nobody's poppet, least of all some pavement cavalier's who had nothing better to do than waste valuable time. With a swiftness born of exasperation she slammed the flat of her hand against his chest and pushed as hard as she could. When the man staggered, she hurtled from him, rushing through the sliding glass doors without a backward glance.

Resuming his journey, Drew Benedict pulled his mouth down into a gesture of amused surprise. Miss Hoity-Toity! Now there was a woman who had not been impressed one iota by his blue eyes and curling lashes. He grinned at the novelty of her disdain, for he rarely encountered such complete immunity to his charm. It was almost as though she had never seen him, but she had. He had looked straight into those grey-green eyes—cat's eyes, he mused—but they had been too busy flashing frosty 'keep off' signals to recognise his grin of appraisal.

He slid into the driving seat of a low Jaguar XJS parked at the kerbside and sat for a minute, rubbing his jaw with a reflective hand. That was the type they needed to deal with the Key Benedict clients. Someone who was singularly unimpressed, who acted well under pressure, who knew the goal in mind and went full steam ahead. The girl had been determined to pass him and even his smile which, in all modesty, he knew possessed a lethal stopping power with the opposite sex, had been icily ignored. The confrontation intrigued him and he arched a brow at the brief notion of what might have been, then he frowned. She was an expensive creature, expensive and doubtless spoiled rotten. Her affluence or, more realistically, her *father's* affluence, shone out in the beautifully-cut lines of her pastel suit, the whiff of French perfume which had tantalised his nostrils, the diamond sparkling on the slender chain around her neck. Full-time employment was not for her. She would devote her time to acquisition, agonising for hours over whether to choose the white grosgrain or the cerise taffeta. He felt a prick of anger as he turned the ignition. The girl was a parasite, a stylish, beautiful parasite.

'First I'll tell you about Key Benedict,' Brian smiled. 'It's a small island, connected to the coast of southern Florida by a bridged causeway, and is in the process of being developed as a select boating and country club community. Three blocks of luxury condominiums are scheduled, of which the first is occupied. There's a hotel, a par seventy-two golf course offering championship calibre play, tennis and squash courts, swimming pools, the usual water sports and a sea-walled marina.'

He glanced up to check if Nicole was impressed, but her expression was grave as she listened.

'And the island belongs to your company?' she asked.

He shook his head. 'We own fifty-one per cent. The Manuel Martinez Corporation originally started the development but were hit hard by the economic recession and ran into difficulties. José, Manuel's son, was a business acquaintance of my brother, Andrew Benedict. They discussed the problem and Drew came up with a proposition. In return for an injection of cash the Martinez family agreed to develop the island on a far more luxurious scale. It was a wise move. Cheaper-priced condos are experiencing a downward trend right now, but luxury properties still command rising prices.'

'I presume the island is called Benedict after the company?'

Brian gave a chuckle. 'Everyone thinks that, but in actual fact a monk named Benedict lived there as a recluse a hundred or so years ago. The name attracted Drew's attention and, I suspect, played a part in his going into partnership with the Martinez family. It seemed a good omen.'

Nicole digested this piece of information, then queried, 'And what role would the successful applicant play?'

'We require a young woman who would be responsible for the sale of ten luxury villas which are almost completed. She'll act as a guide for interested clients, fill a public relations role. Whatever people need to know, she'll provide the information. Sometimes she'll act as an escort on inspection flights, on other occasions she'll chauffeur people around the Key Benedict area to display the advantages of owning a property there. Do you drive?' She nodded. 'Obviously houses in this price range don't attract a continuous flow of customers, so in between times she would be expected to help out at the letting office for the condos. They're selling like hot cakes and the staff are sometimes pushed. Another person to answer the phone or mail out details would be welcomed.' Brian crossed his fingers. 'You say you speak French?' From what the girl had told him so far, she sounded ideal.

Nicole tossed back her hair. 'My mother was French, I'm bi-lingual. I also speak passable Spanish and some Greek.'

At last! Brian thought happily, slumping back in his chair. Someone who matches up to Drew's specifications. 'And you went to university?'

'I gained a two-one B.A. honours degree in Management Studies and French,' she said, eyes now lowered demurely.

Better and better, he chuckled to himself. 'You said in your letter that you have experience of Benedict apartments. Where were they?' He had a shrewd idea they would not be on the Costa Brava.

'We always rented villas, not apartments. My——' There was a split second's hesitation. 'My father preferred a house in its own grounds, he was a stickler for privacy.' She counted on her fingers. 'We stayed in Barbados, Morocco, the Côte d'Azur and Aegina.' Her face clouded. 'Our final summer was spent in a Benedict villa at Puerto de la Cruz in Tenerife.'

Her grave expression worried him. 'Didn't you like it?'

'The villa was fine. There were wonderful views and Charlie, my—my father, used to sit on the balcony for hours.' She gave a vague smile in Brian's direction. 'Unfortunately it revives poignant memories. He—my father died shortly after we left the Canaries.'

'I'm sorry.'

At the troubled rush of recollection which shadowed her face, Brian had the urge to hold her close and assure her everything would be all right, then her mood changed and she was composed again. 'I've been employed on a part-time basis with a firm of travel agents. It was a stopgap job while I sorted out my affairs. I filled a temporary place because one of their staff was on extended sick leave.' She pushed a brown envelope across the desk towards him. 'They were kind enough to give me a reference.'

Phrases like 'quick to learn' and 'excellent manner with the general public' leapt out at him.

'Could you attend a second interview on Saturday?' he enquired.

The open mingling of joy and disappointment on her face made Brian warm further towards her. She was eager to have the job, another point in her favour.

'You couldn't say yes or no, now?' she asked, a trifle breathlessly.

He shook his head. 'Sorry, my brother Drew makes the final decision. The complex in Florida is his baby.' He smiled at her distracted air of alarm and walked round the desk to grin down at her. 'Confidentially, you don't have much competition.'

'Good,' Nicole said delightedly.

One more bend in the lane and then—Honeysuckle Haven! Pushing her spectacles further up her nose, Nicole fortified herself with the knowledge that her journey was almost over, and surely Mr Foster would be kind enough to run her back to the bus stop at the end of her visit?

Although, as the crow flew, the cottage was only twenty miles from her shabby bedsit, it might as well have been on the far side of the moon, she thought wearily, tramping the final stretch. Yet again she wondered what could have possessed her to buy a house miles from anywhere. A car was vital when you lived off the beaten track, but how could she ever hope to afford a car now? With hindsight, the purchase of Honeysuckle Haven had been a vast error, she acknowledged miserably, and yet, at the time, it had seemed the key to her survival. It was well known that doctors advised those suffering from bereavements not to take major decisions for at least six months. Why hadn't she remembered that advice? She knew why. Ever since she was a little girl she had longed for the day when her mother and Charlie would settle down and the three of them would have a proper permanent home. After her mother had been killed she thought that now Charlie would put down roots, but no—the annual cycle from one hotel to the next, one rented villa to another, had continued. His only fixed base had been an office in London which served as a *poste restante* and a business address, and heaven knows what had happened to that since his death . . .

All she had been capable of focussing on when she had been left alone was to find herself a bolt-hole, everything else had been secondary. She had needed a home which belonged to her, which no one could take away. Something solid, buried deep in the heart of the English countryside. Well, her dream had come true! Honeysuckle Haven was hers, she had bought it outright. It was solid enough; the stone walls had stood for hundreds of years, and would doubtless stand for a few hundred more. And the cottage was certainly in the heart of the countryside, hidden so far from civilisation that her feet blistered every time she hiked there!

Like an ebbing tide, her disquiet momentarily receded as she rounded the bend and caught sight of Honeysuckle Haven. Whatever the drawbacks, the cottage was as pretty as its name, with whitewashed walls and sturdy brown thatch. Its charm had captured her heart at first glance and, being a romantic, how could she resist? Although Nicole had first seen the cottage in autumn she had visualised it through the seasons. Snug in the snow, a blazing fire in the inglenook hearth. Then later in springtime a warm breeze would billow snowy-white curtains at the latticed windows while daffodils nodded golden heads in the garden. Come summer the fragrance of honeysuckle would fill the rooms and she would eat delicious home-grown strawberries on the rough-paved patio. She chewed her lip at her lack of foresight. Where was the money to pay for the coal fires, the curtain material, the strawberry plants? It was the potential she had seen, not the reality.

At first everything had gone well. After completing the purchase she had had several thousand pounds in her bank account, money earmarked for furnishings and a small car, but the sum had dwindled alarmingly when unexpected renovations were needed to the thatched roof, closely followed by repair to the ancient plumbing system. After that were bills for paint, carpets, bedding and kitchenware. She had had no idea such modest items were so expensive!

Still, she would have managed if it had not been for the flood. The stream which had tumbled so lazily over the stones at the foot of the garden in autumn had become a roaring torrent in winter. After two months of unceasing rain, which everyone in the village claimed was freak weather, Nicole had awoken one morning to a drowned garden and muddy water invading the ground floor. Although it was only six inches deep, all the newly-bought cord carpeting had been ruined and a mockery had been made of the walls she had so recently and so proudly painted in shades of magnolia and apple-white. When the insurance company advised she was not fully protected, it had been the final straw! Her nest-egg had drained away as rapidly as the muddy waters, and she knew that either she must sell the cottage or find some means of replenishing her bank account post-haste. The temporary position at the travel agents' had seemed heaven-sent, and she had spent weeks combining work with repainting the cottage. But part-time employment was unsatisfactory both from the financial and career aspect, so Nicole had begun searching for a job where she could use both her business degree and her skill at languages. In due course the village grapevine had revealed that a middle-aged couple were seeking a rented house in the area, and Nicole had seen another answer to her problems.

The moment she lifted the latch on the wicket gate, the front door swung open.

'Hello, my dear,' Mrs Foster gushed with such a vivid smile that Nicole inwardly recoiled. 'Do come in. How kind of you to make the effort this evening! Oh, I didn't know you wore glasses, but they really do suit you. You must be tired out after your walk, would you like a drink?'

No reply seemed necessary, for the woman hurried Nicole along the flagged hallway and into the living-room where she reached for a bottle of sherry which had been parked in readiness on the sideboard. The French windows were open wide, and there was a glimpse of Mr Foster, back bent, working at the foot of the garden.

'He's building a retaining wall to prevent any further flooding,' Mrs Foster explained, following Nicole's glance.

She was murmuring her thanks when she realised grimly that she might be asked to pay for the improvement. 'I—I can't afford——' she began.

'Oh no, no,' her tenant chirped, 'he's using stone from a derelict byre along the lane. It's a labour of love, with no cost to you. He's designed the wall to incorporate small flower-beds on top, so you'll be able to plant flowers to trail over the stonework. It should be a most attractive feature.' Pouring two glasses of sweet sherry, she handed a brimming glass to Nicole. 'Cheers!'

Her polite response was wary. The woman's giddy air was concealing something and, with a frown, Nicole looked once more at the distant Mr Foster.

'It must have taken him ages to amass all that stone,' she commented.

The last time she had visited the cottage was three weeks ago when she had collected the rent. There had been no sign of preparations for a wall then, and no sherry ... Her dealings with the Fosters had been minimal. Occasionally they would forward the odd letter or telephone her if one of her university or school friends had tried to get in touch.

'He's been working on it full-time, all day and every day,' said Mrs Foster, sitting upright on the sofa.

Without warning the frivolity dropped away and everything was formal.

'Full-time?' Nicole echoed, her backbone crawling with a premonition of doom. 'But what about his job at the factory?'

'That's just it—he's been laid off. Only temporary, of course, just for a week or two,' Mrs Foster told her, an uncomfortable edge to her voice. 'Things'll pick up again soon. There's a big export order due in from the States and then he'll be back at his machine, doubtless working overtime.' She nodded towards the industrious figure in the garden. 'He won't come in, he feels too embarrassed to meet you, but he wants to know if we could come to some arrangement over the rent.'

There was the onslaught of body-rocking panic as Nicole recalled the tiny amount of cash in her possession. She had budgeted to the last pound, relying on the rent to tide her over until her first salary cheque arrived from the Benedict company—if she landed the job. All hopes of replacing her damaged contact lens drifted into the middle distance.

'What kind of arrangement?' she asked guardedly.

'Would you be prepared to take half rent this time? We'll make up the difference as soon as he's back in work. It's only a temporary setback,' the woman stressed. 'We don't want to leave Honeysuckle Haven, it's such a cosy home, and I know you would prefer to avoid the upheaval of finding fresh tenants. Not everyone would wish to live in such a quiet spot, though it suits us.'

The none-too-subtle reminder that she could find it wellnigh impossible to re-let the house was not lost on Nicole. Mrs Foster was flaying her with a double-edged weapon: unpaid rent and the remote chance of finding replacement tenants.

A bird in hand, Nicole thought cynically. 'I'll agree to one month on half rent, but after that you must pay in full or I shall have no alternative but to ask you to leave.'

She was trying to appear stern and decisive, though inside she was quaking. With luck Mrs Foster would not guess that if her determined stance was challenged it was possible she could burst into tears. Snatching off her spectacles, Nicole rubbed at the bridge of her nose where pressure was proving an irritant. Now her view was fuzzy, and it was a relief to escape briefly from the embarrassing half pleading, half defiant look on the woman's face.

'When my husband has finished the wall, he'll work on the garden,' Mrs Foster offered. 'And if you provide wallpaper and paint he'll be pleased to decorate the bedrooms, free of charge.' She was currying favour, they both knew that.

Nicole replaced her spectacles. It was a tempting proposition and, as she mentally reapportioned her finances, her fingers strayed to toy with the solitaire diamond at her throat. Success with the Benedict appointment would cut out any bed-sit rental, and her living expenses would be paid for by the company during her spell in Florida. But would there be sufficient spare cash for wallpaper?

Lifting her eyes, she saw that Mrs Foster was examining the diamond, and her fingers curved protectively around the brilliant stone. She was being assessed, and Nicole knew that no matter how lucidly she stated her case, the woman would never be convinced that the girl before her could be short of money. Calculating eyes rested on the soft doeskin jacket she had shrugged from her shoulders, and when her designer jeans and white cashmere sweater had been scrutinised, the verdict was clear—Little Miss Rich Girl!

But my clothes are at least twelve months old, she wanted to explain. I haven't been inside a dress shop since Charlie died, and if I could afford anything new I would be searching in the same chain stores as you, Mrs Foster! True, she owned the cottage lock, stock and errant stream, but it was a dubious asset at best. For years it had stood empty until she happened along. Might it not stand empty again before another idiot fell for its picture-book charm? And as for her diamond . . . The slender fingers tensed. The solitaire was her twenty-first birthday gift from Charlie. She had loved Charlie so much, and he had loved her. She would never relinquish his gift—never!

Nearing her destination on Saturday morning, Nicole continued to rack her brains for ways of squeezing out the price of wallpaper from her budget, then her elongated eyes widened dramatically as, rejecting her worries, she swayed beneath the full impact of the Benedict building. Earlier in the week she had been too rushed, and too myopic, to pay much attention. The architect must have been given *carte blanche*, for the tinted-glass walls which swept up into the clouds and the imposing Italian-marble entrance hall reeked of unrestrained luxury. No shortage of ready cash there! she judged wryly.

The building was quiet and her curiosity took precedence over vanity as she strolled through the spacious hall, her spectacles allowing her a clear view of the sumptuous copper and marble décor, the trickle of water over a mock waterfall, cascades of glossy-leaved plants and walls hung with oil paintings which she recognised as being originals, and costly. Nicole walked towards the lifts, raising her eyes to admire a huge central sphere of polished copper suspended high in the ceiling, soft light shining from its Venetian lead crystal trumpets. She summoned the lift and while waiting made a mental list of all she knew about A. Benedict and Company. It was a new concern, relatively speaking, having enjoyed a fast and furious growth over the past ten years. She knew that, in addition to controlling an international portfolio of rental apartments, villas and hotels, the company also financed condominiums and time-sharing schemes in holiday venues all over the world. With a self-mocking smile, she admitted she could use some of their property expertise herself.

'Would you go to Mr Drew's office, one floor up, please?' a girl asked, when Nicole introduced herself on the nineteenth storey.

At the penthouse suite the lift doors slid aside and she scanned an impressive pair of sunburst-design bronze double doors before thrusting her spectacles into her bag. The Benedict boss believed in stylish surroundings, that much was certain! Vaguely she remembered a gossip-column reference to him as a 'millionaire playboy'. He could be a two-headed hunchback for all she cared. She would turn cartwheels to order if he wanted, anything to secure a position in his company.

A final glance to check her outfit. Yes, the soft buttermilk chamois suit with its blouson top and hip-hugging skirt looked good, even though she had first worn it back in her teens. Nicole gave herself a private pat on the back. Over the years she had painstakingly lowered and raised her skirt as fashion had dictated, and her care had now paid dividends. No one would guess that the hem, situated just below her knees, had been down to mid-calf.

Good manners, a pleasant smile, and always tell the truth, a voice warned as she neared the bronze doors. It was Charlie's voice. With a deep breath to calm her leaping nerves, Nicole knocked briskly and at a shouted 'enter', stepped forward to conquer Drew Benedict.

CHAPTER TWO

'GOOD morning,' she said politely.

It was fortunate Brian was near the door, and he hurried forward to shake her hand. Gratefully Nicole smiled at him as he propelled her across the desert of carpet, acting in the unconscious role of guide dog.

'May I introduce my brother, Andrew Benedict, Chairman of the company?' he gestured towards a broad-shouldered figure seated behind a desk in the hazy distance, and Nicole flashed a smile which she trusted was all-encompassing.

Her nerves, already honed to a razor-thin edge by the awareness of how vital this interview could be for her future, began to leap. She was totally adrift. When Brian had interviewed her the room, and his desk, had been compact and he had been near enough for her to make the correct responses. But now! The office was built to the dimensions of an aircraft hangar and the man at the desk was far outwith her myopic range.

Drew Benedict's blue eyes narrowed into instant recognition. So the anonymous Miss Smith was none other than the snooty young woman who had sent him on his way the other morning! He suppressed a grin. Hoity-toity you might have been then, poppet, he thought, but I bet you'll be a little more co-operative now that you want to join my payroll.

'I believe we've met before?' he drawled, peaking a brow.

With a vague smile Nicole sank down on to the chair Brian had indicated which was positioned a yard or two back from the wide desk. 'Oh no, sir,' she replied in crystal-clear tones.

'It was a brief meeting. You had to leave in a hurry,' he jibed, happy to be magnanimous. She really was a good-looking girl.

'We have never been introduced, sir,' Nicole insisted innocently, lifting one shoulder into an elegant dismissal. 'If we had, I would have remembered the name.'

His gaze hardened and he leaned forward, idly stroking his fingertips across the thick moustache as he wondered just what cat-and-mouse game the delicious young creature before him was playing. Since Drew had turned sixteen women had been falling over themselves to attract his attention, his lean six-foot-three-inch superstructure had made it inevitable. True, he had collected a handful of rejections over the years, but never before had he been dismissed quite so coolly, and it rankled.

Brian pulled his chair closer to Nicole, launching into a résumé of the job conditions. 'After a fortnight's training in London there'll be a rota of six weeks in Florida, and one week back here. It could alter from time to time, depending upon when and where clients surface. I'm afraid it could knock the hell out of your social life.'

'No problem. I don't do much socialising,' she assured him, smiling candidly into his eyes.

Brian smiled back.

To Drew, beginning to smoulder behind his leather-topped desk, it appeared they were forming a mutual admiration society, and he didn't like it.

'You don't have boy-friends?' he demanded in a sharp disbelieving voice.

The grey-green eyes skated blindly past his. 'No.'

He frowned. 'Don't your family care about you being away from home for weeks on end?'

'I don't have much of a family.' There was a slight pause. 'Or a home,' she added.

An appealing vulnerability touched her face, but she bent her burnished brown head, the hair swinging forward to shield her expression and when she looked up again the emotion had gone.

Words of sympathetic enquiry which had sprung spontaneously to Drew's lips dried. She's made of tensile steel, he decided, and slewed on to another tack, aware of a malicious need to ruffle this bird's feathers. 'You give an address in the country—isn't that your home?'

'No, not really. I—I have a small apartment closer to town.'

The description stumbled out. It's a white lie, Charlie, she insisted, mentally crossing her fingers. Please understand. Foolish pride would not allow her to admit to a seedy little bedsit in the back streets. Luckily Brian did not notice her moment of unease, and as for the Chairman—well, he appeared to be hunched over his desk, examining her application form.

'Your *curriculum vitae* states that you have only had a few months' employment in your entire life, and that was part-time,' he said flatly.

Nicole detected the stab of censure in his voice. 'Yes,' she agreed, hoping another merry smile in his general direction might stop him in his tracks. It didn't.

'No vacation work during your time at university?'

She shook her head.

'You're twenty-four. There can't be many young women of your age who've never held down a full-time job.'

Nicole was frank. 'I've never *had* to work until recently.'

'Then why waste everyone's time and energy by taking up a valuable place at university?'

There was a look of open scorn on Drew's tanned face, a look which made Brian's blood run cold. His brother could be a sarcastic devil when he wished,

sarcastic and intimidating. He had seen grown men
blanch when Drew glowered and used that derisive tone
of voice—blanch and run. Anxiously Brian turned to
Nicole, but she was unperturbed, her pert profile
composed.

'I don't consider education is ever a waste of time,
even for a woman, sir,' she said sweetly, gazing
somewhere above Drew's head. 'As a matter of fact I
was hoping to join my father's business, but unhappily
he died and——' She wafted a manicured hand.

Drew scowled at the application form. 'I see you
spent a year at a finishing school in Switzerland. Isn't
such an establishment an anachronism in this day and
age?'

Her chin lifted. 'I wouldn't say that, sir. There can't
be many young women of my age who can carve
tomatoes into the shape of a full-blown rose, or know
the correct way to address the Archbishop of
Canterbury, or mix their own mud-pack.'

Touché, Drew accepted wryly, unable to decide
whether or not she was pulling his leg. Did wealthy girls
mix their own mud-packs? he scowled at her, but she
was looking straight through him. Just when he thought
he had contact, those elusive grey-green eyes would
slide away as though he held no more interest than a fly
on the wall.

'Are you sure you want to work?' he demanded,
giving rein to a surge of anger at her blithe disregard.

'Positive, sir.'

The reply was tinged with ice and he saw that, at last,
he was beginning to rile her. He allowed himself a small
moment of triumph. She had spoken evenly, but only
just.

'You can't need the money,' he jabbed brutally,
fixing his gaze on the sparkling diamond at her throat.

Brian's startled intake of breath was audible. 'Drew, I
don't think——' he began, rising to his feet.

There were times when his brother went too far, and this was one of them. Nicole rested a restraining hand on his sleeve, giving assurance that she could cope, and he sank down reluctantly.

'It's a legitimate observation,' she said, a kind of despair welling up inside. So the blurry Mr Benedict harboured the same delusions as her landlady and Mrs Foster! Only strength of will and the knowledge she was perfectly capable of selling his damned villas kept her from storming out, that—and the memory of the meagre sum in her bank account! She cleared her throat. 'I'm sure you understand the value of outward appearances, sir,' she continued, a wintry edge to her voice.

Drew clenched his teeth. If only she would stop calling him 'sir'! She made him feel like an elderly schoolmaster, and now he began to wonder if the term was varnished with impertinence.

'You are aware that in the past my father rented several of the Benedict properties?' she enquired, calmly adjusting the hemline of her skirt over a shapely knee.

'Yes.'

'Perhaps I should explain that the reason he chose your company's villas was because they were luxurious but reliable. They looked expensive, they were expensive, but they were worth every penny—*and so am I*! I believe clients interested in your Florida venture will expect the same high standards, and if you imagine they're likely to buy on the say-so of some little scrubber from West Ham, sir—you're wrong!'

'Am I?' demanded Drew, rising from his swivel-chair to prowl around the desk. Brian was forgotten as he strode forward to confront his slender opponent.

'Yes, sir, you are!' Nicole flared, rising to her feet and summoning up all the courage she possessed to stand her ground. 'You need someone like me. Someone with business training, who is fluent in other languages, who can deal with people from all walks of life. Someone who isn't overwhelmed by a ride in a Rolls Royce, or an upper-class accent—or a millionaire playboy,' she added pointedly.

His dark brows met in irritation. 'I don't overwhelm you, Miss Smith?' he growled.

She gave a casual shrug which left him not knowing what she meant.

'Any newspaper reports you may have read are totally misleading. I'm neither a playboy nor a millionaire. And what's more, I consider my personal life and financial status to be my own business, and no-one else's!' he retaliated. The granite tone indicated the subject was a sore point.

'Money—yours or mine—doesn't interest me too much,' Nicole lied airily, steering the conversation on to safer ground. Forgive me, Charlie, she begged silently, I'm bending the truth again.

A sarcastic grunt indicated that Drew Benedict remained unconvinced, but she ignored him.

'The job you're offering chiefly interests me because I see it as a challenge. It promises to be stimulating. Because I have no home ties I'm free to travel as you require and give the post one hundred per cent concentration. And—and I should be in the sun again,' she added wistfully.

'You enjoy the sun?' Brian intruded.

He, too, had risen to his feet and was stood in the background watching the interplay. The highly-charged atmosphere surprised him. Earlier in the day when they had seen the other girl, Drew had been yawning with disapproval. Now he most definitely was *not* yawning, but neither did he approve of Miss Smith either, it seemed!

Nicole treated Brian to a happy smile. 'Oh yes,' she breathed, remembering golden days from the past.

'You won't be able to spend all your time lying on your back sunbathing in Florida,' Drew said curtly.

He flicked expert eyes over the curves beneath the softly clinging suit—she would look superb in a bikini.

Her heart swelled with relief. 'Then I have the job?' she gasped.

A large hand shot out to grasp her chin. Dammit! he would capture those grey-green eyes if it was the last thing he did.

At the touch of his fingers, Nicole stiffened. For a moment her heart fluttered, but her surprise promptly switched to a more positive reaction. How dared he manhandle her, how dared he! But he was offering her employment and, tempting as it was to twist furiously from his grip, she schooled herself to remain still. Mentally she shot off at a tangent, remembering the last time a man had held her in this way. Then the man had been Roberto, and he had been explaining that as she had no money she could not have *him* either . . .

Money! Her eyes grew dark with resentment. If it wasn't for the sordid fact that she needed this man's money she would have yanked the marauding fingers from her chin and swept from the room.

'The post is yours,' he said. There was a pregnant pause. 'You work on a trial basis for two months, and during that time it's up to you to convince me that you *are* worth every penny!'

Menacingly he bent his head towards her, and as he came into clear focus Nicole stared back dumb-struck. The man had the most magnificent midnight-blue eyes, eyes fringed with sooty black lashes, but they were angry eyes, cold and metallic. He reminded her vaguely of someone she had met—who was it? Thrusting the thought aside, she shuddered. Drew Benedict might have offered her a position within his company, but he didn't like her. There was no attempt to disguise the antagonism tightening his rugged features. The only reason he was employing her was because he recognised she would be successful, but privately he despised her.

Other disapproving faces had worn that look. With deadening conviction Nicole knew he had written her off as a 'rich bitch'.

Brian sat down beside her in the darkened theatrette.

'How are you getting along?' he asked.

Switching her eyes from the screen, Nicole smiled at him. Since her training had begun a week or so ago, the young man had kept a friendly eye on her progress. She suspected he was attempting to atone, in part, for his brother's too blatant disapproval.

'Fine, I think I know the layout of the villas as well as I know the back of my own hand.' She removed her spectacles. 'Clean-lined kitchen and breakfast area with custom-built pale oak cabinets, the counter tops and floors covered in oyster-coloured Italian tiles,' she recited. 'Roman tubs with each bedroom. His and hers dressing-areas concealed behind floor-to-ceiling mirrored walls in the master bedroom.' She glanced up as the audio-visual display rolled to an end. 'Key Benedict occupies a prime location within a water-orientated community,' she chanted in time with the closing words of the commentary. 'It offers luxury, privacy, security—can you afford not to live there?'

Brian chuckled as the images on the screen faded. 'Clever girl! You've absorbed it all. Drew will be very impressed.'

'I doubt it,' she returned crisply.

Nicole had seen the Chairman only once before he had flown off to attend a series of business meetings in some far-flung land, and once had been enough. He had summoned her to explain that on completion of her training she would be acting as escort to a Sir William and Lady Whitman on their inspection flight to Florida.

'Sir William is prominent in the City. He has contacts in both commerce and politics. He could be important to us,' Drew had told her grimly. 'If he decides to buy at Key Benedict it will be tantamount to gaining Royal approval, so don't fluff it.'

'I don't intend to,' she had replied, glaring in the general direction of his tall frame. It was not quite open warfare between them, but nearly.

The spectacles, which had been worn daily, were now left behind in her desk drawer. Nicole was not prepared to have her precarious confidence eroded by appearing before Drew Benedict feeling less than one hundred per cent immaculate appearance-wise. Besides, if she could not see him clearly she was immune to the hostile blue eyes. All she must cope with then was the contempt rolling through the deep voice, though that, heaven knows, made her heart pump a little faster.

'Your brother doesn't like my type,' she said candidly, turning back to Brian and wondering how he could be so approachable when his brother emanated a force-field of leashed anger.

The boyish face flushed with embarrassment. 'You did hit him below the belt at your interview when you implied that he was a playboy.' He chuckled. 'In reality he's anything but. The air was blue when he read that description in the newspaper!'

Nicole wrinkled her nose, recalling a photograph showing the back view of what must have been Drew Benedict with a shock-headed blonde pouting over his shoulder. 'Wasn't he dating some pop singer?'

'Tamsin Jay,' Brian supplied. 'But pop singer is inaccurate, too. She's a high-stepper, sings the blues in posh nightclubs. After their affair was written up in the gossip column she was given the old heave-ho!'

'Why?'

'At heart Drew is a conservative type. He values his reputation as a hard-headed businessman. Until then the only press comment had been financial articles outlining his flair at detecting future trends, his success in building up an international company, all very proper stuff. Being linked with a so-called pop star offended his pride, he's big on respectability.' Brian shrugged. 'The gorgeous Tamsin was shown the door like so many others, not that she was willing to go.'

'Why doesn't your brother get married?' Nicole asked. 'That's far more respectable than having affairs.'

'He was married once, years ago. It was shortlived, luckily there were no kids. Drew will never admit it, but the divorce was a tremendous blow to his self-esteem.' Brian became pensive. 'All our family were knocked for six.'

'But divorce isn't so rare. My mother was divorced— twice,' she burst out, then stopped dead, aware of marching into a minefield.

He threw her a quick glance. 'Perhaps you accept such things, but it was the first break-up in our family's history, and it hurt. At the time Drew was convinced he had ruined his life, and his ex-wife's. That was my mother's reaction too.'

Her mind burning like cellophane, Nicole gave him a smile of commiseration. Her mother's divorces had happened before she was born, but the other break-ups . . . her mother had thrived on break-ups, never caring tuppence for the anguish she caused Charlie as she flew from one affair to the next. Nicole's scalp tightened. She would *not* think about her mother. Unbidden, Roberto came into her head and she winced, remembering the pain she had suffered when he had broken up with her.

'It all turned out okay. Karen, Drew's ex-wife, married again,' the young man continued, his face brightening. 'There was no ill-feeling. My mother regards Karen's daughters almost like proper grandchildren, much to Drew's embarrassment. Invariably she squeezes in a reference to them when she's talking about Hugo's tribe. Hugo is my eldest brother,' he added.

'Is he involved in the company?'

Smiling, Brian shook his head. 'Drew wanted him to become involved, but he wasn't interested. Hugo hates high-pressure living, he runs a small carpentry business of his own. In the early days he helped with the conversions, that's how the company started. Drew bought up old houses and divided them into flats. When business began to spiral Hugo opted out, he's not ambitious like Drew, Paul and me.'

'I've not heard of Paul, either,' Nicole commented. The history of the Benedict clan was fascinating, news of family ties always made her feel comfortable deep inside.

'He's in the Lake District supervising the decoration of some cedar cottages for a time-sharing scheme. He's the youngest of us Benedicts but, like all the company executives, he spends a high proportion of his time away from home.'

'Following in his Chairman's footsteps,' she said pithily.

'Drew should be back next week.' Brian tugged at his ear-lobe. 'I've been trying to persuade him to take a break. He's far too tense. Any little error irritates him these days and then all hell is let loose. He drives himself too hard and gets uptight, but if you can pry him away from work he's good fun. He has a great sense of humour.'

Nicole did not feel she should contradict him, but Drew Benedict—good fun! Doubtless brotherly affection had coloured his assessment.

'Do you see much of each other away from the office?'

She knew she was prying, but the mood was so relaxed that the query just slipped out.

Crossing his legs, Brian lounged into the padded upholstery of the cinema seat, deciding there were worse ways of spending your time than chatting with a pretty girl. Her interest was genuine, and he felt expansive, though if Drew ever learned how expansive, Brian knew he would be hauled over the coals. His brother was tightlipped in the extreme about personal matters. He sighed, recalling previous angry rebukes over what Drew had considered his garrulous behaviour, but why worry? Nicole would be discreet, she wasn't the type of girl who gossiped.

'So-so, but business commitments mean we're often on the move,' he explained. 'Drew, Paul and I each have our own pads, much to my mother's disgust. She wishes we would live at home and she's forever complaining how there used to be a houseful of men, but now she's all alone. My father died a few years ago.' He shook his head in amused protest. 'Mum isn't telling the truth. She's a great one for strong family ties and invariably there's someone staying in the house with her. There are endless friends and neighbours who pop in for a chat, whenever you go the kettle's on the boil and there's someone yattering away nineteen to the dozen.' Brian grinned. 'And of course, there's Sundays.'

'Sundays?' she echoed.

'Whenever any of us are in London we have lunch with Mum on a Sunday, it's a ritual,' he said with a smile. 'Hugo lives round the corner, so he and his wife and kids go regularly, and the other three of us put in an appearance whenever we can.'

Nicole's eyes shone. 'How lovely! It sounds like fun.' If only she had had a family like that . . .

'It is. My mother's a superb cook, so we eat and drink and talk. People come and go all the time. Paul and I take along our current girl-friends, and——'

'What about Drew?' she interrupted, arching a shapely brow.

Brian made a negative gesture. 'Drew has never brought anyone since his marriage ended. Even if he's been deep into a relationship he has chickened out. I reckon he's scared of getting too involved with a woman. My mother's always grumbling about his lifestyle, she says he's too old to be changing his women every five minutes.'

'How old is he?'

'Thirty-six, and he looks every single year,' Brian announced firmly. 'Don't you think he looks jaded? *And* his hair is turning grey.'

'Is it?' Nicole was surprised. The compelling blue eyes had absorbed her complete attention when Drew had gripped her chin, she had had no energy to look further.

'Of course!' The reply contained the lethal confidence of a man five years younger who knew his own black hair was destined to remain black forever. 'Mind you, he's always wanted to look battered around the edges, and now he's achieving it,' Brian exclaimed without preamble.

Nicole raised her brows. 'Battered?' Battered was not a description she would ever have applied to the predatory male animal who had manhandled her and ruthlessly warned that if she didn't match up to his expectations she would be out on her backside.

'He was so damn *pretty* when he was younger, and he hated it,' Brian chuckled. 'When Drew was twelve he tried to cut off all his eyelashes because some kid at school told him they belonged on a girl. Mum was furious! Ironically, when they grew back they were thicker and curlier than before, and she said it served him right.'

'Your mother sounds quite a character,' Nicole grinned, the envy coming through. 'Mine was, too— though not quite in the same way.' Abruptly she stopped. 'I must go. I'm due at Accounts Section for a briefing on how to finance property allied to U.S. legislation.'

Rising to his feet, Brian smiled farewell as she swung away between the rows of plush seats, then his brow puckered. What on earth had possessed Drew to label such a charming girl as a snooty little minx?

The following seven days were hectic. Nicole studied layouts and maps, waded through books, digested facts and figures until her knowledge of the villas, the island and, indeed, Florida was awesome. All she needed now was clients whom she could impress by revealing that Florida had been discovered by Juan Ponce de Leon, a Spanish nobleman, on the Second of April 1513 and that the intra-coastal waterway which separated Key Benedict from the mainland did, in fact, connect the entire eastern seaboard of the United States.

On the personal side she took her courage in both hands and bought wallpaper for the cottage bedrooms, closing her eyes to the expense. She arranged for it to be delivered, together with a note informing the Fosters that she would call for the next instalment of rent in six weeks' time. By then, she tried to convince herself, Mr Foster would have returned to the factory and her money troubles would be over.

Her landlady was disgruntled to discover Nicole was leaving and swung hot and cold over the prospect of her returning at six-weekly intervals. 'You'll have to make do with whichever room is free,' she had warned huffily at last, as though a mile-long queue was clamouring for the shabby accommodation.

As the days flew by Nicole's excitement mounted. She could hardly wait to leave for Florida, and one reason was that when she totted up the ever-decreasing number of pound notes in her crocodile-skin purse, she grew breathless with fear. Never before had she been so poor! But once she boarded the plane the Benedict company would provide her accommodation and food, and what more would she need? Nothing.

She was sitting at her desk on the final day before her departure, fighting to make sense of the electronic security system installed at the Key Benedict villas, when Jenny, the secretary, poked her head around the door.

'The big boss would like to see you,' she said, pulling a face. 'Tread carefully, he's a touch fraught this afternoon, still suffering from jet-lag. He arrived back unexpectedly a couple of hours ago, and judging by the dark shadows under his eyes I'd say he missed his sleep last night.'

'Thanks for the warning,' Nicole grinned, removing her spectacles.

'He says to bring in your passport. He was mumbling something about a multiple-entry visa.'

With a deep breath, she lifted her shoulder-bag. 'Okay, blaze the trail.'

When they reached Drew's office Jenny introduced her and slipped quickly away, whispering, 'Good luck!'

The distance between the bronze doors and the leather-topped desk had doubled since the last time she was there. It was a route march over alien territory. Nicole's heart was in her mouth as she trudged towards the seated figure which had growled a harsh 'Good afternoon'. Hesitantly she waited before him. Drew was in his shirtsleeves, stripped for action, she thought acidly as he stretched out an impatient hand in her direction.

'May I see your passport?' The demand was couched as a request, but it was still a demand.

It was a blessing not to be able to focus on the taut angles of his face. Clearer definition was *not* what she needed, when already her head was throbbing from the muted hostilty in the air.

'Calm down,' she murmured as she zipped open her bag.

The words had been issued as a personal warning to her erratic pulses, and Nicole was as astonished as Drew Benedict apparently was when they rang out clear and precise. Flushing, she bent her head to concentrate on the search for her passport.

'I beg your pardon?' he queried, in a tone of outrage.

He was not prepared to allow the comment to slip by unnoticed, she had never believed he would. The only way was to bluff her way through.

'You seem to be—er—well, a little wound up,' she said, flashing what she hoped was a sympathetic smile. 'I know running a large company must be rather exhausting and——'

She got no further.

'*Wound up!*' Drew thundered, rising to his feet. 'Rather exhausting! Good heavens, what do you know about running a company? The only experience you've ever had is trading merry quips with lecturers over hypothetical problems—and that, let me inform you, madam, bears no relation to the real thing.'

His angry condemnation of her education triggered off a need for self-defence.

'Don't you agree that a degree course helps a person understand the strains and stresses of busines life?' Nicole asked, ordering her voice to remain firm. She would *not* be browbeaten by this monster!

Drew leant forward, palms flat on the desk, his muscled arms as hard and unrelenting as whittled oak. 'We aren't all given the opportunity to indulge ourselves,' he taunted. 'I never went to university. I left school at sixteen and have worked for my living ever since.'

'Oh!'

'Don't sound so shocked,' he jeered. 'I'm not entirely uneducated. I can manage to make sense of the share prices in the *Financial Times* if I concentrate real hard!'

'I didn't mean that,' she protested, feeling her cheeks burn. 'I'm just—well, surprised that you've been so successful so quickly. It's——'

He allowed her no time to finish. 'Don't be so bloody

patronising,' he snapped. 'I realise that to someone like yourself, for whom a major decision in life is whether to dine at the Savoy or the Ritz, my success must appear unbelievable, if not a trifle impudent.' The corner of his mouth curled beneath the dark moustache. 'I hate to disillusion you, but even without the benefit of a finishing school, some of us manage to eke out a living.'

Hostility was flicking from him like blades. Nicole tried to conjure up calming words to defuse the tension, but it was beyond her.

'Passport,' he repeated when she stood mute, and stretched out demanding fingers.

Hot and bothered, she grabbed recklessly into her shoulder-bag. 'Here.' She flung a slim blue book.

With a laugh of scorn he tossed it straight back. 'I doubt even your bright smile would persuade the immigration authorities to allow you into the States on the strength of an *address book*!'

'Oh!' Nonplussed, she stared down at the wedge of documents crowding her bag. Everything was assembled—tickets, driving licence, maps and, somewhere, her passport.

'For Pete's sake!' Letting out a harsh breath of exasperation, Drew strode around the desk, commandeering her bag to produce the familiar dark-blue book with its golden crest.

Mesmerised, Nicole watched as his long tanned fingers switched rapidly through the pages. The moment had gone for her to protest that it was her bag, *her* property, for now he was irrevocably in control.

'The visa appears to be in order,' he admitted, and at the shadow of chagrin he displayed, Nicole felt an upsurge of invigorating anger. So he had hoped to catch her out, had he!

Frostily she took the passport from him.

'Who arranged it for you?' he demanded.

'I filled in the forms and travelled to the U.S.

Embassy all by myself.' Each word was pronounced as
though she was the star exhibit at a seminar on
elocution. 'I completed the various transactions single-
handed. I do possess a modicum of common sense.'

'Good.' The retort was crisp. Drew rested a lean hip
against the edge of the desk. 'How much do you have in
traveller's cheques?' He folded his arms across the pale
grey expanse of silk shirt and surveyed her.

Nicole's large eyes met his in startled confusion.
'Traveller's cheques? I—I mean, I——'

How could she tell him she was unable to afford
any?

'You haven't considered that down-to-earth aspect,
have you, poppet?' he drawled triumphantly, his brow
lifting in an expressive statement of 'I thought so.'

Nicole did a double-take. *Poppet*, Drew Benedict had
said, and with a thud of realisation it hit her that he
must be the man she had so hastily thrust aside on the
pavement when she had been arriving for her first
interview. She had thought he seemed vaguely familiar,
but it had never crossed her mind that the tall
moustachioed figure out in the street could now control
her destiny. Her voice locked in her throat. No wonder
his attitude was so belligerent! She had trodden on his
masculine ego with a satisfying squelch and then
consolidated her error by professing not to have
remembered him. A male as virile as Drew Benedict
would not take kindly to being overlooked.

Interpreting her stunned silence as an admission of
her sins, he appeared to decide that on this occasion he
would act the benefactor. 'I know you profess not to be
interested in money, Miss Smith,' he smirked, blue eyes
gleaming. 'But it does have some uses. Don't forget your
daddy won't be around in Florida to foot the bill.'

'The company pays for my food and accommodation,' she protested, counter-attacking wildly.

'What about incidentals?' he purred, and she saw the

enjoyment he was deriving in making her squirm. 'Don't you intend to despatch one postcard or buy a single tube of toothpaste throughout the entire six weeks?'

Her cat's eyes flashed defiance at the magisterial tilt of his dark head, then swerved aside. He was so smug. He reminded her of Roberto, calm and serene, protected by an invincible shield of all-powerful masculinity.

'I'll manage,' she protested, knowing she couldn't.

'Allow me to provide some dollars,' said Drew, smiling like a Cheshire cat and thus provoking an intense desire to thump him. Strolling back, he removed his wallet from inside the jacket which had been tossed aside and returned to stand before her, patiently thumbing off notes. 'Here's a hundred—don't spend it all at once. The amount will be deducted from your first pay cheque.'

With difficulty Nicole forced out the words. 'Thank you.'

'I trust the arrangements are made with Sir William and Lady Whitman for tomorrow?' he asked archly.

'Yes, they're picking me up in central London and I'm travelling out to the airport with them.'

His brows ground together. 'How come? Why aren't you joining them at Heathrow?' he demanded in an amalgam of wariness and displeasure.

Nicole hid a comforting flare of satisfaction. 'They suggested I join them in their chauffeur-driven limousine.'

'How the hell did you wangle that?'

'I didn't "wangle" anything, Mr Benedict,' she retorted, the tension crackling between them. 'When the Whitmans were at the office last week Sir William——'

'They were *here* last week?' he cut in.

'Yes, I thought they might care to take a second look at the audio-visual presentation, so I telephoned.'

'And who the hell gave you permission?' he flared.

'I wasn't aware I needed permission,' she replied loftily. 'In any case, they were delighted. Lady Whitman said it had all been too much to absorb in one go.'

He was intrigued. 'You struck up some kind of rapport?'

'I believe so. They're a friendly couple, easygoing and enthusiastic. I suspect they're more than halfway sold on the villas already.'

Now she had the courage to meet his eyes without a qualm. His expression had softened, he was pleased at the notion of her initial success with the Whitmans. She gave a tentative smile, and when Drew smiled back she felt the unexpected tug of his charm.

'Good,' he said, the corner of his mouth lifting, and the single word made Nicole glow with pleasure, an emotion she rapidly smothered. He glanced at his watch. 'I dare say you're looking forward to a final evening with your folks. Go home early, if anyone queries it, tell them you have my permission.'

'No need, I'm perfectly happy to work,' she assured him.

It was barely three o'clock and the prospect of long hours alone in her bedsit was daunting. Her suitcases were already organised, so the less time she had to spend waiting around in her dismal surroundings, the better.

'I insist,' Drew coaxed, with a smile which was oddly intimate, and Nicole's heart missed a beat. For the first time she began to understand why Tamsin Jay, his pop singer, had been reluctant to leave, for once the hostility faded he became a most appealing man. 'You'll be going home for final goodbyes?'

She shook her head. 'My country cottage is rented out and my only relation is an aunt who lives in France.'

'*Your* cottage?' Instantly he was on the alert, and the switch to interrogation dismayed her.

'After my—my father died last year I bought Honeysuckle Haven. It's very small,' she added, knowing there was no earthly reason to sound defensive, but that she did.

'And you own a place in town?' Drew swayed back on his heels and slid one hand into his trouser pocket. It was clear the prospect did not meet with his approval.

Visualising the humble bedsit, Nicole decided another evasion of the truth was necessary. If she explained the bare facts—that it was merely rented—she might involve herself in having to reveal the disreputable location and then would fall even further in Drew Benedict's estimation. In reply she gave a small shrug. Her personal affairs were no concern of his, he could think what he liked. There was a long pause in which the blue eyes seemed to lock with hers, searing through her deception.

'The cottage is too remote to travel into London on a daily basis,' she gabbled, annoyed by her need to justify her actions to the critical male before her.

He ran the knuckles of his free hand reflectively over his jaw. 'So you decided to rent out the cottage and buy something else in the city?'

Nicole raised and lowered her hands.

'I trust you realise how fortunate you are to have been born with a silver spoon in your mouth,' he proclaimed.

What a mistake to think he had charm—Drew Benedict possessed as much charm as a boa-constrictor!

'You remind me of somebody's father,' she returned.

'If I was your father I'd make damn sure you realised the true value of money,' he retorted, glowering at the crêpe-de-chine dress she had bought in Paris, the diamond at her throat, the crocodile-skin bag sat on his desk.

Her chin rose determinedly. Nicole had imagined she was becoming paranoid about money—the *lack* of it,

and now this wealthy entrepreneur was accusing her of
having no idea of its value! Irritation, sharp as cats'
claws, scratched her spine. 'I'm sure by the time you
were my age you had money,' she said icily.

'I did,' he agreed. 'But the difference, madam, is that
I had worked for every single penny of what I owned
myself!

Nicole soaked up her surroundings as the barn-sized
Cadillac, José Martinez at the wheel, zoomed along the
expressway from Miami International Airport. Already
thoughts of London and its attendant problems had
begun to fade, the breeze was warm on her bare arms
and the sun had darkened her spectacles into
sunglasses. She grinned happily.

'I hope you guys had a good flight?' José asked, tossing
round a general smile. He was a thick-set, black-bearded
young man with laughing eyes and a friendly manner.

'Excellent,' said Sir William, acting as spokesman.
'I'm usually bored stiff on planes, but today, thanks to
my attractive companions, the flight was a pleasure.' He
beamed at his wife and Nicole.

'Glad to hear that, sir. We trust your entire visit will
prove to be as satisfactory.' José slipped Nicole a secret
wink and she decided she was going to like him.

As he chatted, telling the Whitmans about the local
scene, she allowed herself a few minutes' reflection. The
journey *had* been pleasant. Although the couple were
old enough to be her grandparents, the conversation
had flowed and before they were halfway across the
Atlantic a mutual connection had surfaced. One of her
classmates at boarding school turned out to be Lady
Whitman's niece, and with this bond the formal buyer-
seller relationship was discarded. Now the inspection
flight had an easy holiday feel and they were old
friends.

In retrospect it was ridiculous, but in the empty hours

of the previous night she had been disturbed by a
commotion in the street, and subsequently had lain
awake, palms damp with nervous perspiration, as
nightmarish fears assailed her. Was the harmony she
had felt with the Whitmans a figment of her
imagination? Could it be that, like Drew Benedict, at
heart they despised her! Would they criticise and carp?
In her mind's eye she had seen the flight delayed, the
seats overbooked. No one would meet them at Miami
and, despite the splendour of the brochures, the Key
Benedict complex would turn out to be a shambles!

Sunshine bathed pink and white blossoms of oleander
in the hedgerows, and Nicole relaxed. So far, so good.
Her fears had evaporated, now she *knew* everything
would go right. Advertising boards caught her
attention—happy hour cocktails—T.V. auto banking—
nude go-go—chiropractic clinic—motels and hotels by
the score.

Lady Whitman put a hand on her arm. 'I never
realised there would be such a strong Latin flavour, did
you, Nicki? Look—all those signs on that shopping
plaza are in Spanish.'

The information Nicole had gleaned from her long
hours of reading came into use. 'Many Floridians came
from Cuba or Haiti originally,' she explained.

José grinned. 'Like my pop. He emigrated from the
old country when he was a little kid, yet even now, after
sixty years, he's happier speaking Spanish than
English.'

'But Florida is cosmopolitan, isn't it?' she asked.

'Sure is,' came the reply. 'The sunshine attracts all
sorts. Every year we have thousands of visitors from
Europe, plus folk from every other state in America.
New Yorkers fly down to escape the winter cold, and
we also have our fair share of Canadians.'

'And there's plenty to do?' Sir William enquired.

'You name it, sir, we've got it,' José assured him. 'If

you fancy some deep sea fishing, I'll arrange a launch and we'll take a look for barracuda or marlin.'

'Yes, please!'

'Okay, that's a date,' the young man grinned, turning the car into a spaghetti-junction of expressways and slip-roads. 'We have all the sports—golf, horse racing, a dog track or two, basketball, tennis. For the ladies there are excellent stores, museums, theatres, tropical gardens, Parrot Jungle, the Kennedy Space Centre.' He wound on and on, listing the pleasures his home state had to offer.

'Sounds like fun,' Lady Whitman agreed happily.

José flashed her a wide smile. 'It is.'

CHAPTER THREE

SINCE the beginning of time mankind has paid homage to the sun god, and Nicole was no exception. The caress of the Florida sun was as potent as a sensual lover, making her purr as she lay, half drugged with pleasure, on the balcony of her room. Hidden behind waist-high walls, she had stripped off her bikini top to soak up the golden warmth. A child of nature, Roberto had teased, for she had delighted in the splash of waves on her skin as she swam naked and unashamed.

The sun lifted her beyond the worries which had beset her in England. There, beneath cloudy skies, her problems had been phantom chains tying her to the ground, but here she soared free, like a bird. It no longer mattered that, apart from the money Drew Benedict had provided, she was penniless. The hundred dollars remained intact, put aside to be spent only on essentials. Now the sun had shrivelled her fat plummy worries into raisins and she knew she would get by.

Through drowsy lids she inspected the slender torso and long legs stretched out before her. Once again she had tanned to champagne gold, for she tanned easily, and she gave a satisfied sigh at the knowledge that soon her skin would deepen further to a sultry shade of sweet sherry on ice. An impish grin appeared as she reached for the tanning oil. Charlie would have had a fit if he could see her now! He had never known she had lain barebreasted in the sun, and when she had mentioned the prospect, half joking to test his reaction, he had embarked on a long stern lecture. Fashionable it might be for young girls to drape themselves across the beaches like so many centre-spreads, but not Nicole!

For her to cavort in such a reckless manner deeply shocked his sensibilities. Dear Charlie . . .

Roberto's reaction had been diametrically opposed. As violently as Charlie censored such lassitude, so he had encouraged it and, as she was young and incredibly naïve, Roberto's wishes had swayed her. Charlie's strictures had been forgotten in the face of the Spaniard's whispered flattery. How could she have known that when he had led her to a deserted bay and coaxed her to reveal herself to the sun, and to him, he intended to do far more than admire her curves? The heady exhilaration of showing her body to a man, a handsome adoring man, had swept her on to further thrills. Soon she had become as addicted to making love as she was to topless sunbathing.

Thoughtfully Nicole rubbed coconut oil into her skin. What was the point of puerile longings? Roberto had gone. Doubtless he was now installed as the companion of some wealthy ageing socialite, who could provide the expensive wardrobe and costly lifestyle he craved, in return for his nightly attentions. The grey-green eyes grew solemn as she tried to convince herself that he *had* loved her, after his fashion. Perhaps he had delighted in driving the bright red sports car Charlie had hired for her, and signed Charlie's name to pay for their yachting, water-skiing, the entrance fees and drinks at the fashionable bath and racquet club down the coast, but hadn't he also been eager for them to be alone? Hadn't he climbed up to her room to spend glorious tumbled nights? And hadn't his melancholy brown eyes been damp as he explained that a future for them would be impossible once Charlie was no longer around to provide the cash?

'I'm too proud to be poor, it would crucify me,' he had told her. 'I have no education, no skills. My only assets are my looks and my body; I intend to use them.'

After that brutal honesty Nicole had grown up fast.

She ran her hands over the oiled slopes of her breasts. She, too, had her share of sex appeal, but she would rather die than exploit herself.

Briskly she screwed back the cap on to the coconut oil. Her self-esteem was riding high. That morning Sir William and Lady Whitman had departed with promises of contacting their accountants the minute they reached London in order to arrange the purchase of a Key Benedict villa. At this assurance Nicole had exchanged a wide smile of collusion with José, though privately she admitted their roles had been minimal— the villa had sold itself.

The properties were everything the brochure and slides pledged, and more. How anyone could resist them, Nicole did not know! But she had remained deliberately cool as Lady Whitman rhapsodised over the imaginative multi-layered floor-plan, the whirlpool spa, the patio with barbecue area. For hours Lady Whitman had babbled on about the illuminated wall-to-wall entertainment centre with its television, video recorder, stereo and wet bar, shrieking with delight when her mind switched to consider the exotic theme of natural wood and marble used throughout the house.

Slipping on her darkened glasses, Nicole raised her face to the sun, basking beneath its rays like a smooth brown seal. The days since her arrival had been frenetic, but *fun*, as José had promised. She had taken the Whitmans on tours of the show villa and the other houses, all in varying stages of completion, discussing the advantages of this site or that. The optional extras had been detailed, she had explained the functioning of the sophisticated appliances and later had displayed the width of the facilities the island had to offer. Saturated, they had then travelled farther afield.

José's support was invaluable. He had acted as chauffeur, whisking them off to delightful hidden waterways which Nicole would never have discovered on her own. Presumably he had other commitments, but he had laughingly declared he deserved a break, and when he had taken the wheel Nicole gave a silent sigh of relief. It was ages since she had driven on the right-hand side of the road. One evening José had suggested she take a practice run, but she had been thrown into confusion; at a loss with the automatic gears, the bonnet which stretched out forever, the driving mirror which was never where she anticipated.

'I'd manage, with practice,' she had said, trying to convince herself more than him, but he had laughed and told her to move over.

Squinting at her watch, Nicole saw she had been lying on her back for half an hour and, as a dedicated sun-worshipper, she knew it was time to roll over. Murmuring blissfully, she twisted on to her stomach, but, at the rap of a distant noise, she raised her head to listen; someone was knocking at her door. With a resigned sigh she pushed herself upright and swung into the living-room which, together with a tobacco-brown tiled bathroom and bedroom decorated in lavender and white, formed her accommodation.

'Hold it a minute!' she yelled, tugging on a satin vest.

This would be José, eager to share her gloating delight at the prospect of the first sale. Padding barefoot across the thick curled carpet, Nicole flung wide the door and grinned. The grin faltered. Drew Benedict had beaten the impatient tattoo. Whipping her spectacles from her nose, she stared at him. What was *he* doing here? In her mind's eye she had him tucked safely away, glowering behind his desk in the London office, chain-smoking cigars, his shirt-sleeves rolled up as he answered endless phone calls and dictated memos at three hundred words a minute. Back in London he had been tense and formal, and her eyes widened a little as she took in his appearance. Stone-washed denims had replaced the business suit, denims which fitted tightly, outlining the virile stance of muscled legs set firmly apart. His thumbs were caught into slit pockets at his hips and a short-sleeved shirt, in blue and white check, was unbuttoned to reveal whorls of dark hair on his chest.

Nicole straightened away from the door. He was standing close, too close, and fully in focus.

'I—I didn't expect you, Mr Benedict.'

No answer. The cool blue eyes enumerated her clothing—the brief emerald satin vest which, all too late, she realised was sticking to her oiled skin, and two tiny triangles of white at her hips.

'I was sunbathing,' she said lamely, flapping a hand.

A dark brow arched. 'Indeed?'

'The Whitmans have left. I worked over the weekend, so I'm entitled to——'

'Some free time?'

'Yes. There's a gap before the next clients and tomorrow I shall be working at the letting office, so for this afternoon I thought I'd——'

'Relax?'

'Yes.'

She was speaking quickly, defensively, and was annoyed at herself. Why, when Drew Benedict appeared, did the world spin a thousand revolutions faster, giving her the sensation of clinging on by her fingertips to avoid the drag of G-force? Or DB-force, she thought caustically, for now the animal aggression in his attitude hit her like a blow to the solar plexus. Whatever his reason for being in Florida, he had not visited her merely to pass the time of day, for the metallic blue eyes which slammed into hers were critical—yes, critical!

'The Whitmans have virtually bought a villa,' she announced with an air of 'put that in your pipe and smoke it'.

'Virtually isn't definitely,' he drawled.

Nicole gulped. In bare feet, she felt pint-sized before him. 'Well—no,' she admitted.

'May I come in?'

Without waiting for permission he strolled past into the living-room. Nicole closed the door a little too sharply. She felt like the hired help, and satisfied her need for retaliation by throwing a poisonous glance at his broad shoulders.

Drew jerked his head towards the sliding glass doors and the balcony beyond. 'Carry on sunbathing. I'm well aware acquiring a tan is your prime purpose for being here.'

'That's not true!'

'I hear you subjected Sir William and Lady Whitman to Disney World,' he accused abruptly, catching hold of her arm and steering her into the sunshine, where he pushed her on to the sunbed. There was a jarring rasp of metal on tile as he commandeered a patio chair, sitting astride it, legs open wide, as though mastering an unruly steed. He was positioned like an impatient prosecutor, hell-bent on needling out the truth. His presence, less than a yard away and in devastating focus, made Nicole lick lips that were suddenly dry.

'Explain yourself,' he barked, searching in the pocket of his shirt to produce a crumpled pack of panatellas.

Cross-legged before him, she looked blank. 'What is there to explain?'

An expletive ricocheted around the walled balcony.

'What the hell do you imagine the Whitmans came here for?'

With rapid movements Drew flicked on a gold lighter and inhaled from the cigar until the tip burned scarlet. He was glaring at her through the flame.

'To buy a house,' she said in bewilderment.

'Exactly! *To buy a house*. Not to be carted off to some glorified funfair by a hoity-toity young madam whose main aim in life is self-indulgence.'

Her spine straightened into affronted rigidity, but he had not finished.

'And I understand José drove you there in a Benedict car, and paid for all the tickets, and charged them to *my* company!'

'You've been doing some detective work,' she accused, her lips a tight line in her face.

'You bet I have, and a damn good job, too!' He took a swift angry drag on his cigar. 'You appear to have beguiled José as successfully as you beguiled Brian. They're both so smitten with those cat's eyes of yours that they can't think straight, but don't, for one moment, imagine you can pull the same trick on me!'

'Beguiling you is the last thing I wish to do, Mr Benedict,' she ground out, her chest heaving. 'I have nothing to hide. The Whitmans themselves asked to visit Disney World. They have a brood of grandchildren and wanted to be able to report back. They had a great time, we all did, and as for it being a glorified fun-fair——!' She gave an impatient Gallic toss of her hands. 'Perhaps it is a fair, and it's definitely fun, but the Magic Kingdom rates far higher than coconut shys and a visit to see the bearded lady.'

'I'm pleased to hear it,' he said with heavy sarcasm.

Nicole narrowed her eyes. 'You've never been, have you? You're condemning something you know damn all about, like you condemn me!'

With lazy menace, Drew folded his arms over the back of the wrought-iron chair and rested his chin. 'Tell me about it,' he challenged, gazing steadily from beneath lush dark lashes.

Chin peaking, she glared at him. 'You take me at face value, you have me pigeonholed as a—a rich bitch!'

Now that she had solidified the description into words the sheer lack of justice tightened like a hard band of pain around her chest.

His eyes never flickered. 'Aren't you?'

For a second his implacable conviction disarmed her. Already she had grasped that Drew was not a man to hide behind a façade of social etiquette and white lies, but this frankness was hard to take.

Nicole mowed him down with a glance. 'No! It's true I've had the benefit of an expensive education and spent most of my life untouched by money worries, but why should I apologise? Does that make me unworthy? Okay, so it was my—my father who provided all these—these goodies,' she spat. 'But again I see no need to apologise.' As she spoke, her natural dignity returned. 'However times change. I'm sure you'll be pleased to know that now you could buy and sell me a thousand times over.'

The slim cigar twisted between the long tanned fingers. 'I consider that's immaterial.'

'Why? I can't understand why you frown on me. You are wealthy, so what happens about your children? Won't you want to give them the good things of life?'

'I don't have any children,' he said heavily.

'I know that, but——'

'How do you know? Have you been discussing me?' he interrupted, his face stiff with disapproval.

Nicole was aware she had stepped into a forbidden zone and felt a tiny flutter of guilt. 'I asked Brian to fill me in on the background of the company, and——'

'And he gave you chapter and verse,' Drew inserted, taking a rough drag on his cigar, its fragrance filling the air, blending with the coconut oil and the warmth of the sun.

'He didn't warn me you would arrive on my doorstep and demand a blow-by-blow account of my dealings with the Whitmans,' she replied, feeling a sudden sense of outrage at his intrusion. 'I understood I had freedom to show clients the Florida scene, and as the Whitmans wanted to visit Disney World I saw no reason to refuse. José offered to drive us there in the Cadillac and I presumed he, too, was allowed to make his own decisions.' Clasping her arms around her knees, she tightened herself into a furious figurine. 'If it's the cost of admission that's bothering you, I'll refund the company myself.'

Nicole made as if to rise, realising, with a lurch of her stomach, that the hundred dollars would now be cut by more than half. Drew put a large hand on her shoulder, holding her down.

'No, I'm sorry. I didn't know it was their idea.' He gazed at the tip of his cigar. 'I guess I jumped to the wrong conclusion. And you're quite right, you are free to do what you think best.'

It was easy to see that humble pie did not often feature on his menu and that apologies came hard. Vaguely he glanced around for somewhere to deposit the stub of his cigar, and as Nicole pushed an ashtray across the polished tiles, he gave a lopsided grin.

'Thanks.'

His anger had vanished like snow in the sun. He pushed back the dark hair straggling across his brow with a weary gesture. 'You told me I was wound up. You could be right!'

When he smiled a tiny furrow appeared at one side of his mouth, and Nicole stared at it in fascination.

'You're certainly picky,' she agreed, snapping back to life and risking a grin, for the blue eyes were no longer glacial, they had thawed into wry self-mockery.

He gave a groan of laughing despair. 'That's one of Brian's words—you *have* been discussing me! I'll roast my brother alive when I get back!' He broke off. 'What else did he say?'

This Drew Benedict was no longer the scowling giant.

'That you were battered and going grey!' she declared, throwing caution to the winds.

'Wow! Brothers do great things for your morale.' He

ran his hand into the thick dark waves of hair, tugging a strand across his eyes. 'Am I?' he asked, squinting upwards.

Nicole grinned, her eyes merry. 'There is a little silver at the temples, and as for looking battered, well——'

She tilted her head to one side and paused. Without warning Drew made a grab for her over the back of his chair, pinning her arms to her sides with large firm hands.

'Well what?' he demanded, smiling at her.

Giggling, she twisted her body in a futile attempt at escape, for, judging by the muscles bulging beneath his shirt, she had no hope of success.

'Well, Mr Benedict,' she purred, running the tip of her tongue across her lower lip.

She was being deliberately provocative and enjoying every minute. Flirting in the sunshine was fun and she forgot he was her employer and able to make, or break, her as he wished.

'Call me Drew,' he prompted, and she saw the sun was getting to him, too.

'Okay. Well, Drew, for a middle-aged man——'

'*Middle-aged!*' he expostulated, his fingers tightening on her bare arms. 'I'd have you know I'm in my prime!'

Nicole produced a radiant disbelieving smile. 'Oh yes?'

He tipped himself closer, balancing the chair on two legs. 'Yes, in my prime,' he insisted, his mouth quirking with amusement, the tiny furrow deepening and enchanting her. 'You might be immune to these heavenly blue eyes of mine, but women have trekked across deserts to gaze into their mystic depths.'

'And still do, even now that you're—middle-aged?' she questioned impertinently, the race of her pulses telling her she was anything but immune to Drew's blue eyes.

'With monotonous regularity,' he assured her.

Suddenly everything went very still. He was gazing at her so gravely that her heart turned around. Roberto's dark eyes had been equally expressive when he had lain down beside her on the sand and whispered his love and his desire. Drew's eyes slid to her mouth and on to the rounded swell of her breasts beneath the clinging satin. Hardly daring to breathe, Nicole made herself remain calm, but as his look slurred upwards to linger on her lips, she felt an answering desire.

'Nicki,' he said softly, and leant further forward.

His mouth was inches away, parting to kiss her when, unexpectedly, the chair legs skidded and he catapulted against her, taking the breath from her body as the wrought-iron scrollwork slammed between them. She thrust her hands flat on the sunbed to keep upright, and for a moment his head was buried in the thickness of her hair, his muscular body heavy on hers. There was the raw male scent of sunwarmed skin. Nicole could feel the roughness of the hair exposed in the vee of his unbuttoned shirt, then his fingers tightened and he pushed himself free. Gaining his balance, he swung off the chair with the ease of an athlete.

'A close escape,' he murmured, and her heart thudded as she realised he meant he had escaped from kissing her, for now his manner had switched again. He was cool and urbane, whereas she was all shaken up, pushing her hair into place with trembling fingers.

'I thought you were falling for me,' she said, in an attempt at a joke which didn't quite come off. 'Like Brian and José,' she added when there was no reply.

Drew brushed his fingers across his moustache, and to Nicole it was as though he was brushing aside the memory of the kiss which had never been.

'No chance,' he retorted, with such flat assurance that his words were an insult. She clenched her teeth.

Disregarding her pique, he glanced at his watch. 'I must go.'

'To London?' she asked tartly. 'I understand you jet in and out of airports like a demented bee.'

'A demented *battered* bee?' he questioned with a droll lift of a brow, but when she refused to react he continued, 'No, not to London. I've decided to grab a few days' rest and attempt to unwind. I've moved into the show villa.' There was a hint of mockery. 'I shall experience the good life for a change.'

Nicole was certain he didn't live in a hovel in London, and though she held back an acid rejoinder, her chagrin showed itself in a grumble. 'How can I take clients around when you're in residence?'

'With ease,' he grinned, as they left the balcony to stroll back through the living-room. 'I'm house-trained, you'll be surprised to hear. I promise not to surface from the Roman tub just as you march in to wax loud and long over the splendours of American plumbing.'

Rejecting his low-key banter, she frowned. 'Why can't you stay here at the hotel?'

The prospect of him listening in to her sales pitch was unsettling. She wondered how she could act naturally with Drew Benedict around. For a moment there, on the balcony, she had relaxed, but now her stomach plunged as she remembered how he had never bothered to refute his opinion of her as a 'rich bitch'. The flare of attraction had been only the weakness of a man for an attractive girl, intensified by the heat of the sun and the holiday atmosphere. In future Drew would be strictly on guard.

'The hotel is booked up. I arrived on the offchance, so I'm not complaining.' He strode towards the door. 'As the show villa is furnished down to the last teaspoon, and having been involved from blueprint stage to final conclusion, staying there will give me great satisfaction.' He paused, his hand on the catch. 'And should you need any extra information I'll be within calling distance.'

'I don't require any help,' she assured him. And especially from you, she added silently. Now she wanted him to leave, and leave fast.

'Not even from José, poppet?' he drawled, slowly rubbing the thick dark hair at the nape of his neck.

He was deliberately taunting her, and the fact that he called her 'poppet', as he had done when he had blocked her way on the pavement, was like red rag to a bull.

'He *offered* to help,' she insisted, exasperation flashing deep in her eyes like shards of golden glass. 'I never asked him to do a single thing.'

'You didn't need to. I bet you've never had to ask for anything in your entire life. It's all fallen straight into those pretty little hands, hasn't it, poppet?' he jibed.

Anger flooded Nicole's brain. 'Naturally!' she snapped. 'And it wasn't a silver spoon I was born with, it was a whole damn canteen of cutlery, platinum with diamond-studded handles!'

In confirmation, Drew stretched out a finger and raised the solitaire from the smooth hollow of her throat. 'Like that one.'

With a gasp, Nicole jerked her head away. For a moment his large hand hovered above her breast, then he turned aside and jammed it into the slit pocket of his jeans.

'Get back to your sunbathing,' he told her. 'The men with binoculars will be growing impatient.'

'Men with binoculars?' she repeated in all innocence, but as she read the message in his eyes her cheeks flushed. She was breathing quickly, still smarting from his sneering comments, and the emerald satin was clinging to her uptilted breasts as they rose and fell in taut precision.

'Girls who sunbathe nude must expect a few Peeping Toms or——'

'I wasn't nude,' she cut in quickly.

'Mostly nude,' he amended, his gaze sliding lazily over her. 'A man would have to be blind, drunk or in a trance not to realise there's nothing but smooth bare skin beneath that vest of yours.'

Nicole read criticism in his tone. 'Plenty of young women sunbathe topless these days,' she began.

The furrow at the side of his mouth deepened. 'I had noticed.'

'There's nothing wrong in it.' She glanced round wildly. 'I'm discreet—I'm not offending any of the guests.'

Drew spread his hands wide. 'Did I complain?' he grinned. 'I'm a great admirer of the female form. There's nothing I enjoy better than the sight of a good pair of——'

'Indeed!' she bit out.

Something in his taunting eyes sparked off an urge to challenge that supercilious macho confidence. Nicole remembered how Brian had called him 'conservative', and, crossing her arms over the flat stomach, she curled her fingers around the lower edge of her satin vest. Locking defiant eyes with his, she began to peel it slowly upwards. How would the mighty Drew Benedict react to the sight of her sun-golden body? He was a mere male, when all was said and done. After his initial surprise wouldn't he gather her up in his arms, like Roberto, and promise to be her slave forever? And then, when he was her slave, she would make him pay for those sneering jibes about her background—a background which had been beyond her control.

But as the satin was pulled higher, revealing silky golden midriff, her bravado faltered. The tall man watching her was *not* Roberto. Roberto would have been smiling, his dark eyes glistening at the prospect of the delights to come. Instead Drew was calm, self-contained, lounging a wide shoulder against the door. The provocative upward drag of satin ceased.

'Carry on,' he purred into the oppressive silence. 'I'm longing to see your suntan, I'm sure it's quite spectacular.'

For a moment which seemed like eternity, Nicole stared up into the cool blue eyes, wondering what madness had spurred her into this unbelievable action. Surely the sensual recklessness was not something in her genes, something she had inherited from her mother! *No!* she dismissed the idea. Roberto had been her only lover. Before, and since, she had acted with decorum, following Charlie's teachings. Drew Benedict would have been only the second man to behold the thrusting firmness of her young body, though she realised, with a wave of self-disgust, that he would never believe her. In addition to 'rich bitch' he must now have added 'wanton' to his opinion of her, and she couldn't blame him. Miserably she pulled the vest down to her waist, lowering her eyes, unable to face whatever she might read in his expression.

'You appear to have a dose of Florida fever,' he commented, and Nicole swallowed hard, gulping on a ball of shame which was in danger of choking her. 'Perhaps you've been wound up like me, that's when it hits you the hardest,' Drew said softly. 'It's a combination of long hot days in the sun and the American air of "let it all hang out".' He chuckled. 'You can take that whichever way you wish.'

His tone was gentle, and when she forced herself to meet his eyes she discovered, to her amazement, that he was not condemning her—indeed, he seemed to sympathise.

'Florida fever is dangerous for us staid souls from England,' he continued. 'You get so you don't give a damn. It creeps up unawares and you suddenly realise you're laughing a little louder, playing a little harder, drinking three glasses of wine where two would have been plenty.'

He was giving her a way out.

'The wine,' she lied, flashing a weak smile of gratitude. 'That must have been it!'

There had been no wine. With the fanaticism of a teetotaller, Nicole had refused to sample the contents of the bar in her room, or ask for an aperitif in the restaurant. True, the company collected the tab for her board and lodging, but whether this included such items she did not know, and had no intention of risking unnecessary expense. She preferred to use her salary for more urgent items, such as new contact lenses.

Crawling back on to the sunbed, she wondered if there was some truth in Drew's mention of Florida fever. Back in London being without contact lenses would have tormented her, but here she was content to manage. Surely José had noticed how her spectacles grew light and dark as she went in and out of doors? But he did not seem to care, and neither did she. Nicole chewed her lip. She still cared about Drew's reaction. He might despise her expensive background and rich girl aplomb, yet in part he had hired her for her style, so appearing before him in spectacles was impossible.

Again she wished he was not installed at the show villa, he was too close for comfort. Why had he decided to take a holiday now? Here? Brian had said his brother had not bothered to have a break for years. Worriedly she sucked at the tip of a lacquered nail. Had he come to keep an eye on her, to assess her performance in selling his precious villas? No, she was over-reacting. It was foolish to suppose Drew would take time off to investigate the actions of a mere cog in his vast organisational wheel.

Wasn't the fact that he had hired her proof enough he considered her fit to represent his company? Somehow she was not convinced. His furious path to her door over the Disney World visit was indication enough that she was first in line for his criticism. So he was tense and overworked, perhaps he had acted impetuously. Nicole pouted. She refused to believe a few days in the sunshine would unwind Drew Benedict sufficiently for him to reassess his low opinion of her.

Sitting upright, she pulled off the satin vest. Why should she worry? If he chose to join her landlady and Mrs Foster in their bigotry, then that was his prerogative. She didn't give a toss. From now on, Nicole decided, she would act the 'rich bitch' if that was what he expected and metaphorically push his face into a custard pie by selling every single one of his damned villas.

At nine o'clock sharp the next morning Nicole was installed behind the reception desk of the letting office, handing out leaflets to holidaymakers who had fallen for the tranquil charm of Key Benedict, and endeavouring to answer their questions. Frequently she was forced to beg help from Rochelle and Jean, the girls who ran the operation, but they gave it goodnaturedly, grateful that she was willing to plunge in head first, and do whatever was required.

The crush eased off around ten, when everyone disappeared towards the beaches or marina, and then there was time to chat between enquiries, and an opportunity to get to know one another. Like José, the two girls accepted her with no questions asked, teasing her a little about her accent but, in typical American fashion, caring not one jot about her supposed status on the social scale.

Both blonde and buxom, they were friendly young women with a great capacity for giggles and gossip, though the office was run with brisk efficiency. Nicole was able to relax and the hurt which had pricked since her encounter with Drew started to dissolve.

'Here's that handsome José,' Rochelle trilled as the

young man came into the air-conditioned office. 'There's nothing I wouldn't do for you, oh light of my life,' she giggled as he feigned a blow at her chin.

'Sorry, babe, not right now,' he said. 'It's Nicole I want.'

'Gee, superseded by an imported model!' Rochelle complained, but she winked to show she was joking.

'A French-Canadian family have arrived en masse from nowhere to take a look around the show villa,' José explained, getting down to business. 'Can you come and do the honours?'

When they were driving down the wooded lane which led to the bay and the villas, Nicole found herself fussing with the slashed neckline of her pale linen dress.

'Is Drew around?' she asked offhandedly.

José swung the Cadillac on to the red-brick drive. 'Haven't seen him. I guess he's taken off for the day, and so he should. That guy needs to go native for a while, introduce some wine, women and song into his life.'

'All work and no play?'

'You said it.'

He braked alongside a huge Buick crammed with expectant grinning people.

'Have a nice day,' he said, waving a cheerful farewell as he pulled away to leave Nicole in charge of her clients who were pouring into the imposing entrance hall of the villa.

'*J'ai grand plaisir à vous souhaiter la bienvenue à la villa d'exposition de Benedict,*' she began, and an elderly man, the patriarch of the family, beamed approval.

'You speak French!'

She grinned. '*Ma mère était française.*'

'*Ah oui!*' he exclaimed, and proceeded to rattle away, explaining how, although his family knew English, they preferred to speak French. By the time they had reached the bedrooms Nicole had been introduced to each member of his large family and had settled easily into her second language.

As she stepped over the threshold of the master bedroom she hastily scanned the interior, but all was in order. There had been no trace of Drew so far, and here only a paperback thriller on the ivory marble bedside table indicated that the room had an occupant. Swinging back to her audience, Nicole began pointing out the plentiful closets, the subdued murmur of the integral air-conditioning. She had swept a graceful arm towards the bathroom when, without warning, the door opened and Drew strode out. He halted when he saw he was not alone and for a moment looked blank. Surprise, closely followed by acceptance, chased across his face and then he smiled.

'Excuse me,' he said. 'I wasn't aware there was a viewing appointment fixed for today. Please allow me to introduce myself, I'm Drew Benedict.'

He gave Nicole a tepid smile, making her aware she was wearing her glasses which, by now, had surely lightened to ordinary lenses. Hurriedly she took them off.

Drew shook hands with everyone, even down to the smallest child, and began to explain how he came to be in residence. That he was clad only in brief white shorts, with a fluffy towel hung around his neck, did not appear to faze him at all. If he hadn't stepped directly from the Roman tub, he had just been shaving, for there was a trace of white foam on his moustache which he towelled away. Nicole felt a flare of resentment at his unexpected presence, but the French-Canadians were delighted, especially the women. Indeed they were smiling in rapt attention, drinking in every word he said and rolling their eyes over the husky contours of his chest.

'The house is wonderful, but we need more space,' the patriarch explained. 'As you can see, we are a large family and we enjoy holidays together.'

'That's no problem,' Drew smiled, dabbing droplets of moisture from his shoulders as he launched into a detailed explanation of how some vacant sites had been kept aside to accommodate custom-built villas which would be constructed to blend in with others on the development.

After standing like a spare part for several minutes, Nicole began to smoulder. This was *her* domain. Drew had no right to interfere. When a hiatus came, she broke into rapid French, suggesting that on completion of their tour of the villa the family might care to visit the vacant plots.

'*Merci, mademoiselle,*' the patriarch responded, and gabbled on in French, tossing glances and including Drew in the conversation, though there came no reply.

Nicole threw him a sideways look. He was faking it well, appearing interested, but suddenly it dawned on her—he didn't understand a single word. *Drew Benedict could not speak French!* She nearly laughed out loud. Now it was his turn to smoulder, and Nicole began to enjoy herself, making small jokes where everyone laughed uproariously and Drew forced out a lukewarm smile.

His only excursion into French was '*au revoir*' when the family, plus Nicole, piled into the Buick to visit the vacant sites. As they accelerated away she flashed a smile through the car window and was rewarded with a furious scowl. She might have discovered a chink in his armour, but despite her temporary elation, she had a feeling she could be the loser in the long run.

That feeling intensified when, having waved farewell to the French-Canadians, she discovered she had left her information folder back at the villa. Her stomach knotted. The folder was her bible, not something to be left around for a cleaning woman to lose in a hidden corner. Retrieve it she must, and promptly. With determined steps she retraced her path to the villa, keeping her fingers crossed that, by now, Drew had disappeared for the day.

She had her own key, but just to check that the house was empty, she rang the bell. When the door jerked open instantly, her legs turned to jelly. Drew stood there, and what she saw in his eyes scared her. In automatic response she dragged the darkened spectacles from her nose.

'So, you've returned to the scene of the crime,' he taunted, somewhat melodramatically, she thought.

'I don't know what you mean. I've come to collect my folder—I believe I left it here.'

As she entered, Nicole glanced vaguely around. The furnishings in the living-room where in the palest shades of pearl interwoven with a hint of mauve, and she realised that her folder would be camouflaged to perfection. She was taking another step of enquiry further into the room when firm fingers landed on her shoulder, restraining her.

'Not so fast,' drawled Drew, swinging her round to face him. 'I want an apology and an assurance that you won't pull that trick again.'

'What trick?' she questioned, distracted by the urgent need to locate her folder.

'Speaking French when you know damn well I don't understand!'

Playing dumb seemed to be the only way out. 'Don't you?' she gasped, her eyes wide and innocent.

'Cut it out,' he snapped. 'I wasn't born yesterday.'

'The clients preferred to speak French,' she said, quaking a little as she admitted that Drew was not fooled, nor ever likely to be.

His face darkened with annoyance. 'Maybe, but you could have explained at the outsct that *I* don't speak it.'

'You could have explained that yourself,' she returned, flipping back her hair.

'How? It all happened so quickly. You were

jabbering away, laughing and carrying on as though you'd all been bosom pals for years, and everyone appeared to think I was in on the joke. I would have looked a complete idiot if I'd suddenly bleated out that I didn't have a clue what was happening.' He gave a snort of disgust.

'You carried it off very well,' she said, and suddenly hysterical laughter bubbled in her throat. 'You deserve an Oscar.'

'And you deserve a bloody good smacked bottom!' he growled, but as the metallic blue eyes slammed into hers Nicole could restrain herself no longer.

'It was so funny!' she exclaimed, and swayed in his grasp, rocking with merriment.

Drew held himself stiff, struggling to maintain the aura of outrage, but her chuckles proved contagious. 'Oh, women!' he sighed, admitting defeat as he, too, began to grin.

'I bet those French-Canadians imagine you have fluent French,' she crowed, weak with laughter. 'What'll you do if they come back and want to speak to you?'

'Hide in a closet!'

'His or hers?'

'The broom cupboard under the stairs.'

Nicole chuckled again, but as her amusement calmed she became hotly aware that Drew was still wearing only the brief shorts, and the chest she was resting against was bare and muscled, covered with black curly hair. Abruptly she dropped her hands and took a step backwards.

'I—I came for my folder,' she said weakly.

Drew jerked his head. 'It's over there.'

It was no use staring blindly into space where everything looked the same. 'Where?' she demanded, needing more direction.

'There!' he said impatiently.

'I can't see it.'

With a hiss of exasperation he put an arm around her shoulders and swung her slightly left. '*There!* Are you blind or something?'

'Thanks.'

Nicole still couldn't spot the folder, but she was not going to tell Drew that. She was taking a hesitant step forward when his fingers clamped around her upper arms and he swung her back to face him. His eyes narrowed into black slits.

'You can't see it, can you? You're so bloody shortsighted that you can't see it!' At the note of victory, Nicole squirmed in his grip. 'Oh, poppet,' he drawled smugly, 'I don't reckon not speaking French is half as chancy as not being able to see.' He held her firm. 'Why don't you use your spectacles?'

'I—I don't like them. I usually wear contact lenses, but they've torn and——'

'Why don't you buy new ones?'

'Have you seen the price!' she burst out, and Drew raised his brows in silent surprise. He chuckled.

'Come on, Nicole, just how shortsighted are you?' He pushed himself back, tanned arms straight, fingers now curled around her shoulders. 'There—am I in focus?'

'Yes,' she snapped, not wanting to join in his game.

'And how about here?' he asked, stepping closer.

'Yes,' she said again, shaking her head to bring an end to his tormenting.

His voice was low. 'And here?'

When he had shaved he must have cleaned his teeth, for his breath was minty. His eyes were suddenly serious, his teasing forgotten. Pushing a hand into the richness of russet hair at the back of her head, he captured her, forcing her to be still.

'And here?' he murmured, bending his head to brush his mouth across her lips.

Nicole felt a rush of desire at the gentle caress. 'Yes,'

she breathed as he paused, as if deciding whether or not to clinch the kiss.

'Nicki,' he said roughly, on an intake of breath, and his mouth became insistent.

She found herself sliding her hands across the living bronze of his chest, seeking support from his hard body. The movement of male muscles beneath her fingers was as potent as an aphrodisiac, one which Drew, too, seemed to taste, for his mouth became more demanding, parting hers with consummate skill. As his lips moved over the edges of her mouth, teasing and tantalising, she stirred, her fingers spreading across the mat of dark hair, her body blossoming like a flower at the first touch of spring.

Drew caught hold of her hands, bringing them up to twine around his neck before he pulled her closer, holding her so tight against the full length of his body that she could feel the burn of his skin through her dress. Her own temperature began to soar as she strained against him, head spinning deliriously with the excitement of the moment. It had been so long since a man had held her, and the pressure of the hard body against hers, the eager probing of his mouth, was sending her slightly crazy.

He began a more comprehensive exploration beneath the cover of his kisses. One large hand deserted her shoulders to slide firmly away on a voyage of its own. Pausing for a slow moment, it caressed the contour of her spine before gliding on to her ribcage. His mouth moved sideways, kissing a heated path to nibble seductively beneath her ear, his thick moustache whipping her skin into flamy submission. Nicole caught her breath, teetering on the brink of passion as his fingers slithered between their bodies to close around the swell of her breast, its peak already tight with desire.

'Nicki!'

Drew's breathing quickened as he struggled to master the excitement rising between them and transform it into something he could handle. He buried his face in the gleaming tumble of her hair.

'Why you?' he murmured vaguely.

Crystals of awareness exploded in Nicole's head and her thought processes whirred into action. Drew was no lover. He was a—a hater of her, or at least of the type of girl he believed her to be. A tempting female body was the sum total of what she represented. Florida fever must exist for he seemed to have forgotten that, at heart, he despised her. Her brain must be fevered too, for why else was she succumbing so readily to his caresses? She pushed against his shoulders.

'Isn't that—er—isn't that José's car? I heard the horn. He said he'd come and collect me, and I think he's here now.'

Breathing raggedly, Drew stood back. His mouth lifted into a wry smile. 'You might be as blind as a bat, poppet, but you're red-hot on the hearing! Why, I'd lay bets José hasn't driven away from the letting office yet.'

Nicole schooled her features. 'I really did hear him,' she lied in earnest. Animal instinct warned her a speedy exit was vital. 'See you around,' she said, hurrying for the door.

Drew chuckled. 'See you, poppet.'

CHAPTER FOUR

BURNISHED head bent, Nicole examined the contents of her coffee cup with an undue show of interest. It was mid-afternoon and Rochelle and Jean were using the break for a lighthearted discussion of men, with a capital M. José and several other specimens had been reviewed, and now, inevitably, Drew's name had arisen. Since she had made her escape from the show villa the previous day there had been no further sign of him—or her folder—and as the two girls plunged into a giggling précis of his effect upon them, Nicole's face clouded. If only there was some way of retrieving her papers, yet avoiding Drew . . .

'A Tom Selleck look-alike,' Rochelle declared, rolling her eyes in exaggerated admiration.

Rochelle had a mania for shackling everyone up to a celebrity. Nicole wondered whom she was supposed to resemble but had hesitated to ask, fearful the answer might prove less than flattering. In her spectacles she privately classified herself as a schoolmarm spinster, but she was not prepared to risk hearing that description from anybody else. The self-criticism prompted her to drag the offending spectacles from her nose.

Jean pursed her lips in consideration. 'I guess he has the same jock equipment of six-foot-wide shoulders and dreamy eyes, but he's more insular. Always keeps his distance.'

'Huh! that's because he doesn't get to Florida too often, and when he does he's tied up at the site office with architects and construction guys,' Rochelle rejoined. 'If he was here permanently, like José, he'd loosen up.'

Nicole was unable to resist a comment. 'But never *that* loose!' she grinned. 'Drew is English, dammit. Stiff upper lip and all that.'

The two girls chuckled.

'I guess you could be right. He is a far more private person,' Rochelle conceded.

Nicole preferred him that way. If she was honest José's ultra-casual manner grated at times and she bit back a smile at her own English reserve. Despite being Resident Director, a position of prestige, José bounded around the island in worn cut-offs and a towelling shirt, shouting, 'How ya doin'?' to all and sundry. Nicole did not want him to abandon the 'laid-back' approach entirely, but felt a little more propriety would be in keeping.

She rose, collecting the empty cups to take them through to the tiny kitchen at the rear. Her know-how with the condominiums was still far from perfect, so she compensated with do-how, fetching and carrying in the hope that her contribution would ease the load.

Rochelle smiled gratefully as Nicole reached for her cup. 'You look so different without your specs—real dishy. You have gorgeous eyes. Why don't you wear contact lenses?'

'I did,' she confessed. 'But I damaged them and now—well, to be honest I can't afford replacements until I draw my salary on my return to England. There'll be two months' money waiting then, so I'll buy new ones straight away.'

'Why wait? I'll loan you the cash,' the American girl offered immediately. 'There's a fantastic vision centre across the causeway. They would make up your prescription within twenty-four hours, or might even have the correct lenses in stock. Go along now.' She lifted the phone. 'I'll ask José to drive you there.'

Nicole held up a hand. 'Wait, wait!' she pleaded,

laughing at such riproaring enthusiasm. 'It's a kind offer, but I can manage.'

Abruptly her mind flashed to the lost folder and her subsequent entanglement with Drew—a direct result of her myopic state. Noticing the shadow of doubt, Rochelle leapt in.

'Why manage when there's no need?' She dialled José's number. 'It's a crime to imprison those lovely eyes behind plain old specs!'

The entire episode was accomplished at such breakneck speed that Nicole had no say in the matter. Within minutes José arrived in the Cadillac to hurtle her over the palm-tree-lined causeway to the mainland. Parking outside a shopping precinct, he steered her into the vision centre where she explained her predicament to the head optician. The man whisked her through to a consulting room and when the tests had been rapidly accomplished, he checked his stock and produced lenses which met her exact requirements.

Little more than an hour after their departure, José flung wide the door of the letting office and, with the flourish of a conjuror producing a rabbit from a top hat, carolled, 'Here you are, folks—the irresistible woman!'

Rochelle and Jean clapped their hands in glee as Nicole attempted to express her thanks and relief. In the end, lost for words as gratitude bubbled from her, she hugged them both, and when José demanded, 'Me, too!' she hugged him as well.

It was not only the new lenses which had brightened her world, it was knowing she had friends. Since Charlie and Roberto had disappeared, her life had been starved of affection, and such openhearted warmth filled an aching gap. She beamed with pleasure.

'How about making up a tennis four this evening?' José suggested, lolling against her desk. 'Rochelle and I usually play with Jean, and Mike from Maintenance, but Jean can't make it.'

'Have to visit an aunt who's having a birthday,' the girl explained.

'I'd love a game,' Nicole smiled, then her face fell. 'But I don't have tennis whites.'

She had noticed that one of the rules on the board adjacent to the tennis courts stipulated correct wearing apparel. The rule amused her, for throughout Key Benedict holidaymakers strolled around in anything from grass skirts to boiler suits, and it seemed odd that once you stepped on to grey shale convention ruled supreme.

'We can stretch a point,' José grinned. 'Tee-shirt and shorts will do fine, so long as they're not too vivid. We'll meet at eight. The courts are floodlit and it's cooler if we play when the sun has gone down.'

Twisting to examine her rear-view in the mirror, Nicole decided her tee-shirt would do—just. It was white, one point in its favour, and matched her cotton shorts with their navy trim—the only problem was the slogan on the back. In copper-plate writing it asked, *'Voulez-vous coucher avec moi ce soir?'*

Roberto had bought her the shirt, though he could ill afford it. He had been amused that while Charlie had stolidly protested about the risqué question which hung between the shoulder blades of his precious Nicole, *he*, Roberto, was assured of an affirmative answer whenever he whispered the words into her ear.

She pulled a face. From a distance the slogan blurred into a navy rectangle, no one watching from the sidelines would be able to distinguish its meaning and, having no alternative, she gave it a mental go-ahead.

The sky was inky-blue when she greeted José and Rochelle beside the tennis courts. Figures in blinding white darted around under the glare of floodlights, some grimly intent on the game, others squealing at their ineptitude.

'Mike had to take a rain check,' said José, making Nicole straighten up from examining the racquet Rochelle had provided and raise questioning brows. 'Drew's joining us,' he explained.

Her heart performed a somersault and collapsed in a heap, but somehow she kept her voice steady. 'That's nice, is he a good player?'

José tugged speculatively at his beard. 'He reckons not, says it's years since he last played.'

'Thank heavens,' she cut in. 'I'm rusty, too.'

'With those shoulders he'll have a service like an express train,' Rochelle prophesied as Drew arrived to join them, and a covert glance at his powerful physique in the white tennis shirt and shorts inclined Nicole to agree.

'Hi!'

His grin encompassed the three of them with no special attention to Nicole, a fact which strangely peeved her.

'Had a good day, Drew?' José asked, as they walked towards their court.

'Great. I went fishing and struck lucky. I caught several dolphin.'

'Dolphin!' Nicole gasped, and promptly wished she had kept quiet.

Only seconds before she had been deciding her best bet was to maintain a low profile, but his comment had drawn a spontaneous outburst.

'Dolphin,' Drew repeated firmly, his features spreading into a smile as he looked down at her. 'But not the Flipper kind you're imagining. It's a gamefish which lives only in warm salt waters. It can grow to six feet and weigh up to a hundred pounds, though the ones I landed were much smaller. You'll find it in the restaurant here on the island, it's a lean fish with a delicate flavour.'

'Oh!' was all she could think of to say.

'I'll partner Drew,' Rochelle declared, and José slung an arm around Nicole's waist.

'Right on, babe. It's you and me together, we'll beat the you-know-what out of them.'

'Fine,' she agreed meekly.

Rochelle served first and, more by good luck than good management, Nicole returned the ball with a certain degree of panache. By the time several points had been played, she was starting to enjoy herself. Yes, she was out of practice, but she had been a useful player in her time; a member of the school team, and sometimes playing with Roberto and friends in Tenerife. José lavished encouragement, which helped. He was quick to shout, 'Well done, partner!' and 'Great shot!' when her serves hit target. A strong energetic player himself, he poached one or two balls which strictly she should have played, but probably would have missed.

Last to serve was Drew, and as Nicole faced him across the net, she told herself to beware. His assessment of his ability had been modest in the extreme, for, despite being somewhat erratic, he exhibited a natural flair and was capable of returning backhands and lob shots with shrewd accuracy. He had kept himself in fine physical condition, and moved with ease, reflexes alert. On occasions he misjudged and slammed the ball into the net, but Nicole was aware that Rochelle's prophecy was destined to come true, his service *would* be dynamite.

Thwack!

Before she had time to react, something whizzed past to thud against the chainlink fence behind her.

'Wow!' José murmured in an undertone of admiration.

Nicole had made no move at all.

'Was it in?' Rochelle shouted.

José nodded emphatically. 'Oh yeah, it sure was in!'

'Did you see the ball, Nicole?' Drew asked.

The taunt made Nicole realise that, of course, he was not aware she was now wearing contact lenses. Initially her play had been hesitant, which Drew must have attributed to shortsightedness rather than a lack of practice.

'Yes, I saw it.'

With difficulty she kept her face straight. She might have lost the point, but in their own private game she felt she had an advantage. José was demolished with the same unplayable service, but when her turn came again the first ball hit the net, and the second was softer. Two hands gripping the racquet, Nicole lunged forward and the ball shot back to land within an inch of the baseline and beyond Drew's outstretched arm.

'Great shot!' José exclaimed, and though common sense told her it was a fluke, she began to entertain heady ideas of her own prowess.

When the doubles match was over, she and José scraping to victory, it was this inflated ego which made her nonchalantly agree to play Drew at singles.

Nicole served first, winning the game by hitting the ball obliquely, so that it trickled over the net as, milliseconds too late, Drew thundered towards it. After watching for a few minutes José and Rochelle drifted off to find a drink, denuding her of their encouragement and, it seemed, her luck. Each of Drew's services hurtled past, leaving her breathless, and she had gained no further points when she came to serve again. This time he had mastered her sneaky technique and returned the ball with a mean top-spin which was beyond her control.

Another game of his high-octane serves—no points— and the puffy elation whined away like a pricked balloon. Nicole began to seethe with frustration as one quick-fire ace after another was slammed at her, for Drew gave no quarter, aiming at her backhand, which was her weaker stroke. Roberto had never been so merciless, she grumbled to herself, chasing after another ball which she hadn't the remotest chance of returning. Hotter and stickier by the minute, she found herself running back and forth across the court until she could have wept from sheer exhaustion.

'Six-one,' Drew announced as he shot back a final lob.

Nicole made no attempt to run—what was the point? She wanted to snarl that it wasn't fair. Drew had been establishing his male supremacy, and had chewed her up, relishing every mouthful.

'Want another set?' he asked, tilting his dark head as he met her at the net.

He looked disgustingly fresh and energetic, whereas she was sweat-sodden, like a wet rag. Panting, she denied the challenge in his gleaming eyes.

'No, thank you. We should give the others a chance.'

José and Rochelle had just returned. At least they had not watched her annihilation in total, she thought, walking towards them. 'Drew won six-one,' she announced before he could boast of his brilliance.

'You did very well—considering,' he drawled, giving her a smile of such dazzling patronage that her teeth ground together.

'Considering she's a woman?' Rochelle chuckled. 'Oh, you male chauvinist pig, you!'

He grinned. 'Considering she's been playing in the dark.'

As stars were needling the black sky, his comment made sense of a sort, though Nicole knew he was referring to her supposedly shortsighted state. Reaching for a towel, she rubbed away the rivulets of sweat from her arms and legs.

'You look drained, are you okay?' Rochelle asked.

She gave an answering nod. 'I think I'll pack in now, if you'll excuse me.'

All she wanted to do was crawl off and lick her wounds.

'I'll walk you home. I'm pretty whacked myself,' said Drew, taking her arm. He smiled at José and Rochelle. 'Have a good game, you two.'

'I can see myself home, thank you,' Nicole muttered, waving goodbye and managing to disentangle herself from his grip at the same time. She lifted the damp hair from the back of her neck and sighed. 'It was hot under those floodlights.'

'You're dehydrated, you need liquid,' Drew told her, frowning at her.

They turned from the glare of the tennis complex, plunging into the velvet mantle of the night. The service lane was deserted, only a breeze in the sea-grape bushes disturbed the peace. Nicole studied the roadside plants—fleshy pods of cacti, serrated coleus, all spattered dark with silver-black shadows.

'We'll have a drink at the villa,' Drew decided when they reached a crossroads.

She stopped dead, tugging at the waistband of her shorts. 'Thanks, but I'll go straight on to my room, I can have some water there.'

'Water? I had something a little more exotic in mind. How about a Piña Colada? I'm an expert when it comes to cocktail shaking.' He saw she was unconvinced and added. 'That folder of yours is still with me—don't you need it? I understand another British couple arrive tomorrow.'

'Oh—yes,' Nicole admitted, the uneasy knowledge that he was keeping track of her workload filtering through.

She shifted from one foot to the other. Lethargy was creeping over her and suddenly she felt too tired to argue; agreeing with his suggestion was the easiest way out.

'You play excellent tennis for someone who can hardly see the ball,' he commented, adjusting his pace to match her plodding steps as they turned into the lane which led to the bay.

Nicole allowed herself a small smile in the darkness. 'I've been cheating—I can see. I brought a new pair of contact lenses this afternoon and I'm wearing them now.'

Her hair was all over the place, and she began smoothing it with her fingers, pulling damp tendrils from her cheeks.

Drew's stride faltered. 'You told me you didn't have any money.'

His voice was hard and she knew that, once again, he was condemning her. His lack of trust made her want to snivel.

'I didn't,' she replied. 'Rochelle was very generous and loaned me enough to buy the lenses.'

'You hardly know the girl!' he cut in.

Nicole cast him a sidelong glance, but the branches which met overhead made it too dark to read his expression.

'I hardly know you, and you lent me a hundred dollars,' she replied flatly, denying the wearying lurch of her emotions.

'That's different—I'm your employer. You should have come to me.' He sounded hurt and angry.

Pride would never have allowed her to ask the critical Drew Benedict such a favour, for the fewer inadequacies she revealed to him, the better.

'How many other people have you borrowed from?' he demanded, making Nicole squeeze shut her eyes to force back the tears. The ruthless tennis had reduced her to a pulp and still he was intent on grinding her beneath his heel. 'Rich bitch', 'wanton' and this evening 'money-grabber'. She didn't think she could take much more.

'No one,' she said, choking on the words.

'I'll pay back Rochelle and you can owe me the money,' he growled.

The independence which she had clung to since Charlie's death now seemed futile. This man was barging into her life, holding her to ransom, and she was helpless against him. Shaking her head from side to side, Nicole refused to look at the tall figure beside her.

'No, Drew. It has nothing to do with you.'

His derisive grunt made her sniff with misery.

'You're not crying, are you?' he asked, leaning over her, and all at once his voice was gentle and his presence protective.

It was the unexpected concern that demolished her. Had his disdainful anger continued she could have held on to her control, but the note of anxiety reminded her of Charlie—how he had worried about her—and, without warning, crystal-bright tears spilled down her cheeks.

'Nicki, don't. You're worn out, that's all,' he said, stopping to pull her into his arms and crooning words of comfort as her head nestled against his shoulder. 'You're right, the contact lenses are none of my business. I shouldn't interfere, forgive me. Brian reckons I'm an overbearing bastard at times, and I am.'

It was like having Charlie back again as he held her close and rocked her, and stroked her hair. For a few minutes she leant against him, wallowing in the cosy cocoon he provided, but Charlie would not have been capable of swinging her up into his arms and carrying her down the length of the lane and into the villa.

'Stay here and I'll fetch your medicine,' Drew ordered, setting her carefully down on to an overstuffed pearl suede couch, and kissing her forehead.

Nicole lay there like a chastened child, dabbing away her tears and deciding that she might have misjudged him.

There were three glasses on the tray he brought back.

'First you must drink this,' he said, sitting down

beside her. Suspiciously Nicole eyed the pale green liquid. 'It's a health drink formulated to replace the natural salts you've lost by exercise,' he explained. 'That's what has thrown you off balance.'

'Is dehydration a symptom of Florida fever?' she asked in an attempt to make him smile, for his eyes were dark with worry. She was successful for Drew visibly relaxed, relieved she was recovering.

'I dare say, though Florida fever is a devious complaint, the symptoms can vary.' He watched as she took a tentative sip. It didn't taste too bad. 'Drink it all up, there's a good girl, then you can have the house speciality—Piña Colada à la Benedict.'

'I thought you couldn't speak French?' she teased between mouthfuls.

He gave a lopsided grin. 'Limited phrases!'

When Nicole had drained the health drink, she escaped to wash her face and tidy her hair. After that she felt much better and her natural poise had returned when she joined him again in the living-room.

'I've had Piña Colada before, but this is delicious,' she said, grinning at him as she sucked at the straw. Drew had served the drink complete with fresh fruit slices and a juicy red cherry. 'What's the recipe?'

'The usual rum, pineapple juice, coconut cream, plus a special ingredient that wild horses couldn't drag from me.' He arched a brow. 'Or even wild women— correction, wom*a*n.' The blue gaze which met hers was heavy with meaning.

'I—I didn't really intend to strip off the other day,' Nicole protested. 'I just wanted to shock you.'

There was a slow disbelieving, 'Yes?'

'Well, you're conservative,' she justified. 'And—and I must have had too much sun.'

'*I'm* conservative?'

'And battered,' she teased.

'And middle-aged?' Drew moved closer on the couch,

resting an arm along the backrest behind her. 'Tell me,
how come such a battered, middle-aged specimen
managed to beat you hollow at tennis this evening?'

In the light of his smile the trouncing took on a new
slant. He had played honestly, to win, and what was
wrong with that? Nicole's lower lip jutted, her grey-
green eyes dancing. 'Okay, you're not battered and
middle-aged.'

'Two down, one to go.' Drew deposited his glass on
the faux-malachite table before them. 'I can disprove
conservative too.' There was a disturbing look in his
eyes.

'How?' she asked, suddenly wary.

'By answering the question on your tee-shirt. Yes, I
will sleep with you tonight.'

He meant it, she knew. Fire and ice swept through
her body, arousing a desire which was as unexpected as
it was violent.

'Is that one of your limited French phrases?' she
asked, playing for time as she plucked up her senses.

The furrow deepened at the side of his mouth. 'One
of the most useful.'

'I believe you—you're not conservative,' she agreed,
sucking so wildly on her straw that when loud noises
indicated that the glass was empty, she was surprised
and thrust it aside in embarrassment. 'I'd better go,' she
gabbled, but the way he was looking at her was melting
her bones and movement was impossible.

Lazily he leant forward, running his fingertips
across her smooth cheekbones and into her hair,
curling his hands to cup the back of her head and
pull her close.

'You have beautiful, beautiful eyes,' he murmured,
his breath warm and sweet on her face.

Nicole didn't know what to say, but she had to say
something. If she sat still and accepted the kiss that was
parting her lips she knew exactly where she would end

up—in the master bedroom, showing him her spectacular suntan.

'Ditto,' she said pertly. 'I believe you cut off your
eyelashes once?'

The spell was shattered, and Drew released her, a
sigh marking his dissatisfaction at her flippancy.

'Why don't you compile my biography? You seem to
know so damn much about me,' he said, but his smile
took the sting from the words. He straightened. 'Fancy
another drink?'

It made more sense to say 'No, thank you,' and head
for the door, but fever was befuddling her thoughts
and she did not want to leave him—yet.

'Please.'

Nicole ambled after him into the kitchen, needing for
some strange reason to keep him close, but why? Maybe
the long months of living alone had caught up with her,
and now it was company she craved? But *Drew's*
company? The casting was all wrong. So his presence
made bands play loud music in her head, but that was a
physical thing. Once, with Roberto, it had been enough,
but now she was older and wiser, she hoped, and
needed more. Basically Drew did not approve of her, no
matter how much he wanted to hold her close and kiss
her, so there could be no future. But did that matter?
For now was not it simply enough to be with him?

'I loathed being cute when I was a kid,' he grinned,
mixing the ingredients for their fresh drinks. 'I always
drew the attention while poor Hugo, my elder brother,
was ignored. You could say it's because of my "cuteness"
that I've ended up running a multi-million-pound
company while he remains a self-employed carpenter.'

She frowned. 'How come?'

Drew dropped a red-striped straw into each of the
tall iced glasses. 'We had an aunt, and, true to form, she
fussed over me, but was lukewarm with Hugo. When I
was seventeen she died and left her house, a rambling

old place, to me—to me alone! Not to my parents, or to
Hugo as the eldest son, but to me!' He rubbed a hand
across his brow. 'It still makes me feel guilty, even after
all this time.'

'And what happened then?' she asked, leaning her
elbows back on the counter to listen.

'My first reaction was to sell up and either give the
proceeds to Hugo, or split them between the entire
family, but Hugo swore he'd never touch the money—
that it was mine. Eventually I decided to modernise the
house, turn it into flats. I'd worked as an apprentice
electrician since I'd left school and been involved in a
similar scheme, so I knew how lucrative it could be.
However, the main purpose was to involve Hugo. I
persuaded him to work with me and we did the
conversion at weekends and in the evenings because we
couldn't afford to give up our regular jobs. When it was
completed the house was sold at a good profit. I paid
Hugo over the odds for his work and he accepted the
money—grudgingly, but he did accept it.'

'Then?' she prompted.

Drew paused, reliving the past in his mind. There
was a wry chuckle. 'Then I was left with thousands of
pounds which no one in the family would accept
because now they reckoned it was legitimately mine,
having worked all the hours God had sent on the
damned house, so——' he lifted his hands into a gesture
of resignation, 'I purchased another rundown property,
and Hugo and I repeated the conversion.'

'What about plumbing and decorating? Did you
employ outsiders to do that?'

He shook his head, several strands of dark hair
wafting across his brow, imparting a rakish air. 'No. I
borrowed a stack of do-it-yourself manuals from the
local library and waded through them.'

'Self-taught?' Her wide eyes showed her admiration.

Drew laughed. 'I can assure you that on numerous

occasions I nearly blew it. Some of the early houses were disaster areas, we met hundreds of snags we'd never anticipated.' He lifted a broad shoulder. 'Fools rush in etcetera, etcetera, but the gods were kind. Gradually I began to employ tradesmen to do the conversions for me. I embarked on property speculation farther afield, then become involved in the holiday accommodation scene, and—here I am.'

'Sounds easy,' commented Nicole, mentally adjusting it to 'sounds brilliant'.

'Success has its price,' he warned, eyes suddenly serious.

As she followed him back into the living-room, it clicked that he was referring to his broken marriage. If only she dared ask him about that, but she knew the limits. The reason Drew was talking so freely was because her tears had dissolved the barrier between them, but private areas remained, areas into which it would be foolhardy to trespass.

'Wasn't it possible your aunt left the house to you because she recognised that you were capable of putting her assets to good use?' she remarked, sitting down beside him on the sofa.

'I doubt it,' he said drily. 'She only saw the blue eyes, not the real me. People are dazzled by superficiality.' He gave a mirthless bark of laughter. 'Hell, in this life if you're reasonably attractive and earn a bob or two everyone presumes you've got it made.'

Nicole's breath caught in her throat at the irony of his words, for surely he was describing his reaction to *her*! But he was frowning, dark brows gathered close, intent on his own train of thought.

She took a long cool pull at her drink. 'You're over-simplifying matters. Isn't it more likely your aunt knew you had the drive and ability to go farther than Hugo?'

He scowled, still unconvinced.

'Don't sell yourself short,' she insisted.

The corner of his mouth twitched. 'I'm sure your years of experience enable you to impart such worldly advice, madam!'

It was a mild rebuke, and she could tell he was not prepared to believe her just yet.

'You employ thousands of people, create their livelihoods, and provide holidays for thousands of others. Is Hugo capable of doing that?' Nicole demanded, driving the point home.

Drew burst out laughing. 'Okay! I confess, I'm bloody marvellous. But enough is enough, now let's talk about you.'

'Me?'

Nicole was knocked askew. Drew's story—his family ties—had caught her imagination and now, abruptly faced with her own background, she felt inadequate. Drew's roots were strong. His marriage may have been a failure, but he knew where he belonged. There were people who loved him, who cared about him; he was a secure member of a robust and respectable family, whereas she . . .

'There's not much to tell.' She searched around in her memory for something to say, then her face brightened. 'We had some wonderful summers in Benedict villas.'

It was a red herring, thrown out in an effort to divert attention.

He took a final swig from his glass. 'Which house did you rent in Puerto de la Cruz?'

'It would have to be the most expensive in your brochure! Charlie—my father, always believed in having the best money could buy.' Briefly she wondered if she should soft-pedal her past affluence, but rejected the idea. Why should she? 'It was magnificent, Spanish-style with red-tiled roof and white walls. You followed a long drive through the pine forests on the slopes of

Mount Teide, and there it was! There was a wonderful view of the coastline for miles around.'

'And your mother was there, too?'

Wings of russet-brown hair shielded her expression as she bowed her head. 'No, she was killed in a car crash a year or two previously.' Nicole had no wish to talk about her mother. 'The villa had huge gardens,' she added chirpily, but Drew was following a different track.

'Do you have any brothers or sisters?'

'No.' She swallowed down the remains of her drink.

'Where were you born?'

'In England. My father was English, my mother French.'

'Whereabouts in England?'

He was becoming too inquisitive, and panic made her catch her lower lip between her teeth. Perhaps Drew *was* conservative. Perhaps he would not understand the irrationalities of her past. It was a risk she could not take. His enquiries must be avoided, but how? Charlie's condemnation of dishonesty forbade her weaving a web of lies.

'Do we have to talk so much?' she murmured, nuzzling into Drew's shoulder.

Fingers widespread, she slid her hand slowly across his chest and was rewarded when his muscles tightened and he grew still.

'Nicki?' A brow, half curious, half amused, lifted and the furrow at the corner of his mouth took shape as he waited to see what she intended to do next.

Edging closer, Nicole curved a hand around the back of his head, swaying with such tantalising grace that when her fingers plunged into the gipsy-dark hair her body brushed against him. Drew waited no longer, but hauled her directly into his arms, bending his head to claim the soft questing mouth. Nicole knew she was playing with fire, but what alternative had she? The kiss was deepening beyond her control, the insistence of the mouth which mastered hers making her heart slip and slide. And yet, in the dim recesses of her mind, she knew one kiss would not be sufficient, that she was committed to following through. Her rough strategy was working—too well—yet she dared not allow more questions. She purred and wriggled closer.

'Have you any idea what you're doing to me?' Drew groaned, and raised her upturned hand to his lips, kissing the palm with a half-open mouth. The touch of his lips on her skin was electric, and as he steered her back into the over-stuffed suede cushions until she was almost beneath him she knew the high-voltage charge had caught him, too, for what she was doing to him was etched in the hard male thrust of his body. Again his mouth possessed hers, his kisses becoming more and more passionate until it seemed he was intent on invading her, desperate to absorb her very soul.

'Oh, Nicki!'

Beneath her outstretched hand Drew's heart was pounding like a jungle drum, and, hardly knowing it, she tugged wildly at the buttons of his shirt, sighing when they were freed. The rasp of the dark whorls of hair against her fingers swept away the last vestige of a deliberate seduction. No longer was she the seducer, she was the seduced. Drew tugged her tee-shirt free fom its anchorage and she moaned softly against his lips, arching her back when his hand claimed the smooth swell of her breast. She was riding a rainbow that soared to the heavens.

Drew wasn't satisfied. After a moment he lost patience and peeled her tee-shirt and bra away, a low animal sound issuing from deep within his throat at the sight of her sun-ripened body. Reasoned thought had vanished. Now Nicole was aware only of textures, sensual textures—the smooth rub of suede on her naked spine, the roughness of Drew's hairy chest against the tips of her breasts.

'Darling,' she muttered brokenly as his thigh separated hers. She was weak and panting, her breasts swollen with desire as he dragged his palms upwards across the honey-brown peaks, making her shudder as an explosion burst deep inside her. His dark head bent further, the bristles of his moustache rasping erotically across her burning flesh until she was suspended somewhere between the moon and paradise. It was the clarion call of the telephone that brought her to her senses. Heart racing, she steered his head from her breast.

'The phone,' she gasped.

'No, no.'

Stubbornly he shook his head, refusing to relinquish the delights of her body. Nicole pulled away.

'The phone, Drew!'

He looked dazed. In slow motion he stretched out a hand, fumbling with the receiver until he finally succeeded in dragging it to his ear. 'Brian?' He raked a hand through the black tumble of his hair. 'Oh, *Brian*!'

Now he was functioning again, and Nicole used his reluctant transfer of attention for escape. When he put his hand over the mouthpiece and ordered 'No!' she faked a laugh and continued to dress, stemming an urge to obey his demand. Drew controlled too much of her life already. She would not allow him to control her heart too, not when she was aware of his true opinion of her. Briefly she closed her eyes, summoning up the pride she would use to keep a wedge between them. Her headlong flight into his arms gave him the right to add 'tease' to his insulting opinion of her, but even that was preferable to revealing the truth about her background. Kiss him she would, but she would not allow him her complete surrender—a surrender he would doubtless count as to be no more than expected from a *girl like her!*

Decent again, she spotted her folder and jammed it beneath her arm. With half an ear on Brian's conversation, Drew was now glowering grimly at her hurried retreat, and it took all of Nicole's *savoir faire* to toss him a vivid smile and march out of the door.

The next morning found José eager to discuss their game of tennis and Drew's part in it, but Nicole kept her replies brief, instead taking an exaggerated interest in her surroundings. They were on their way to the airport to collect the new clients and when a small plane droned above, she thrust her head out of the car window, damming the conversation mid-stream.

'Char-broiled steak dinners at five-ninety-five plus free all-you-can-eat salad bar,' she read on the banner trailing behind. 'Sounds like a bargain,' she commented.

José was easily distracted and now switched to a summary of American cuisine, taking great relish in pointing out the 'Lousy Food and Cold Coffee' restaurant when they reached Miami. A wide variety of eating places lined the roads—everything from hamburger joints to elegant bistros—and Nicole had endless opportunities to keep the conversation flowing. She giggled at the novelty of a sign advertising 'Hot dogs steamed with beer', though José assured her they were great and said that one evening he would treat her to some.

Simple as it was to sidetrack the young American, when she neglected the attractions of the passing scene Nicole experienced queasy waves of self-disgust. She must have reached rock bottom in Drew's estimation, for he would have quickly realised that her quest for his kisses had been contrived, at first, and, despite the heat, she shivered.

It was something of a relief to discover that Mrs Purdy, the dominant half of the couple she was to introduce to the villas, was an addicted talker. Now there was no time to ponder on Drew and his opinions.

Harlequin reaches
into the hearts and minds
of women across America
to bring you

Harlequin American Romance.™

YOURS FREE!

GET THIS BOOK FREE!

Twice in a Lifetime
REBECCA FLANDERS
Harlequin American Romance

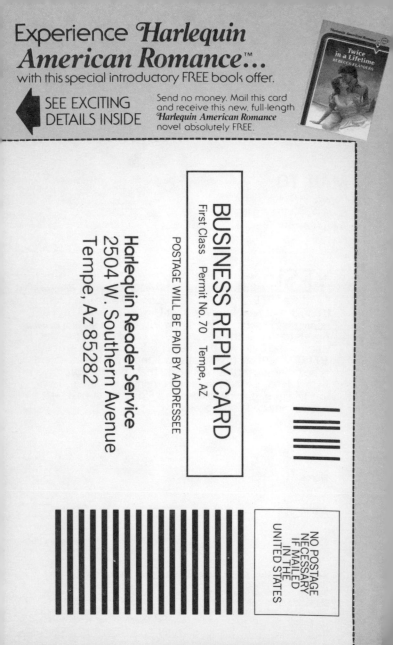

Nicole was forced to devote her entire attention to non-stop questions, observations and a mash of extraneous chatter and spent the rest of the day living on nervous energy in an attempt to keep one step ahead of her client. Mr Purdy hardly uttered two words, but his wife . . .

Even the vivacious Mrs Purdy proved susceptible to the strain of a trans-Atlantic flight and subsequent tour of Key Benedict, however, and had wound down to a halt, opting for dinner and a quiet night, though how she achieved anything quietly Nicole hadn't a clue.

The red message button was lit on the telephone when she returned to her room mid-evening, and her pulses quickened. For a few rash moments she wondered if it could be Drew, but no, it turned out to be José, breathing words of praise and congratulation. Brian had called advising that Sir William and Lady Whitman had now signed on the dotted line, and the sale was definite.

'Drew's on his way round to see you,' José chortled. 'Aren't you a clever kid!'

'And he's happy?'

She hoped the good news would cancel out some of her so-called sins. Perhaps if she were to explain that she preferred not to mix business with pleasure Drew would accept her abrupt withdrawal the previous night.

'Over the moon,' José confirmed. 'We'll have to crack open the bubbly, babe.'

He chattered on, tying her to the phone when she was itching to get away and freshen up before Drew arrived. Her ice-white two-piece of waistcoat and A-line skirt edged with gold was creased from sitting in the car. In England she had slipped a blouse or sweater beneath the waistcoat, depending on the temperature, but in the balmy air of Florida she wore it alone, her tan creating a stunning contrast.

She had dropped down the phone, ready to dash and

change, when there was a knock at the door. It was too late now to do more than summon up a degree of self-confidence and she crossed her fingers hopefully behind her back.

'Hello,' she said with a wary cheerfulness as Drew paced into the room. It was impossible to read his expression and she closed the door to join him, her heart swinging like a yo-yo. Clearing her throat, she took the initiative. 'José was on the phone, he said the Whitmans had signed. Are you pleased?'

He turned away to stare through the window at the blue Atlantic beyond the sand-dunes. 'Yes, thanks very much.'

His diffident response intensified her guard.

'You're really pleased?'

'Ecstatic.'

He didn't sound it. Nicole watched, pulses fluttering, as he slumped down on to the sofa, and, with a sigh, leant forward to rest his elbows on his knees. He bent his head, rubbing his jaw with the palm of both hands as though reaching a decision and then, having made it, his head jerked up and his blue eyes hooked on hers. The emotion in the taut set of his face was anything but ecstasy, and propelled her into a protective step backwards.

'I've been at the site office all day,' he said, and Nicole registered that he was formally dressed in a navy shirt and toning trousers. 'After our conversation last night I started to think. Your mention of the long let of the villa in Puerto de la Cruz rang a bell, a series of bells, so this morning I sent some telexes. The name Smith threw us at first, perhaps you can explain that, or perhaps you can't, it doesn't matter. The point is that when you and Charles Werner left Tenerife a year ago you also left behind a stack of unpaid bills.' He rose to his feet and towered above her, freezing her with the icy slash of his eyes. 'Including one for three thousand pounds. Money which you, madam,' he jabbed a threatening finger under her nose, '*you* owe to my company!'

CHAPTER FIVE

NICOLE's brain locked solid. For a moment she was incapable of thinking, of moving, then an avalanche of white rage swept over her. She no longer cared that Drew's feelings about her were ambivalent, that was something she could handle, but for him to demean her beloved Charlie, to besmirch a dead man's memory in this way . . .

Fists clenched at her sides, she was trembling with fury. 'How dare you! How dare you accuse Charlie! He always paid his way. He was a man of high moral principles and I won't have you suggesting he would stoop to anything so—so low!'

The skin tightened across Drew's cheekbones. 'Your father may have——'

'He wasn't my father,' she snapped.

'Stepfather, then,' he said harshly. 'He may have persuaded you he was whiter than white, but believe me, he owes one hell of a lot of money back in Tenerife.'

She gave him a withering glance. 'Rubbish! There's been a mistake, crossed wires somewhere. It's a sore point with you that I've had a—well, an affluent upbringing, and for some reason you're using this—this preposterous charge to try and——'

She ran out of words and ideas, for what she was saying struck her as unreasonable. Whatever Drew was, he wasn't petty and, she thought uneasily, he was not a liar. Flinging her arms into the air, she gathered speed.

'I have no idea what this is about, but I can assure you Charlie always settled his accounts before he moved on.'

Drew let out a hiss of impatience. 'Not the last time!'

'But he rented Benedict properties for years, your records must show he was reliable,' Nicole protested.

'He was—in the past. Which is why our man in Tenerife agreed that he could settle his account on departure. Normally the rules are prior payment, but in this case——' Drew rubbed the wide-angled jaw with tanned fingers, 'in this case we should have known better. Werner dropped us in it, right up to the neck!'

With a ragged gesture Nicole brushed the fringe from her brow. 'You must have confused him with someone else. Honesty was a religion for him, he would never have left without paying. Your facts are wrong *wrong*!'

'Spare me the denials,' he commanded, in a voice devoid of emotion. 'I haven't fathomed out yet what your role is here, but there's a police report which lists all the firms who supplied Charles Werner with services and goods last summer. Like us they were left high and dry and, like us, they suffered. Debts as steep as his precipitate bankruptcies. Being cheated out of three thousand pounds is no joke, I would have nailed him if I could, but he skipped out of the island and covered his tracks.'

'That's a lie, he didn't skip out!' she cried, nostrils flaring. 'He was an old man—old and sick. He wasn't capable of skipping anywhere.'

'He was capable of holidaying in the sunshine.'

'At the beginning,' she was forced to agree. 'But one day he was soaked in an unexpected downpour and he caught a cold. It developed into something far worse. Within days he was coughing all day and all night, he was fighting for his breath. I brought in a doctor——'

'Yes, he has an unpaid account, too,' Drew inserted.

'He maintained it was a chill, but Charlie knew differently,' she said, her voice cracking. 'One morning he asked if I would mind if we cut our holiday short and left.'

Drew's expression never altered, his eyes were trained on her like a hawk assessing its prey. 'Where did you go?'

'To London. Charlie was terrified at the thought of dying in a foreign land, he was desperate to return to England.'

'Sounds an ingenious excuse for leaving in double-quick time!'

Taken aback by the acid insinuation, Nicole felt her cheeks burn. 'All right, so we *did* leave in a hurry, but that doesn't prove anything.'

'It proves your creditors were hot on your heels!'

'*No.* Instinct prompted Charlie to get back to his homeland, he was like a wounded animal making for a burrow. He knew time was running out.'

'Precisely! The pressure had become too great. If you hadn't got the hell out of there he, you, or possibly both would have ended up in gaol,' Drew announced flatly.

The brutal words wounded her like a machete, but she soldiered on, logic taking over from raw emotion.

'Your information must be wrong. No one ever mentioned unpaid accounts to me. Charlie had a spotless reputation, everyone liked him and trusted him.'

'Did you handle the financial side?' Drew probed.

Nicole bit her lip. 'No,' she admitted in a small voice.

'So you have no evidence to prove his innocence, and yet the police have plenty which proves his guilt.'

'But he was wealthy. Over the years he supported my mother and me in great style.' Her grey-green eyes were troubled. 'My mother didn't come cheap.'

'Did you?' he questioned savagely, leaning back against the sofa. 'Your education must have cost a pretty penny.'

Nicole let his jibe pass, now was not the time for justifying *her* life. She shook her head in bewilderment, russet hair swinging on her shoulders.

'There was never any hint that his finances were anything but secure,' she stressed.

Drew sighed, stretching out his long legs. The fury of his personal attack on her was draining away, and he raked the hair from his brow with weary fingers. It seemed she had convinced him of *her* innocence, but what about Charlie's?

'Where did Werner's money originate?' he questioned.

'He dealt in the commodity market.' She paused, watching his reaction. 'It was all above board,' she added in defiance.

Thoughtfully Drew ran his tongue across his lower lip. 'Commodities? That can be a gambler's game. Did he run his own company?'

'I—I don't know,' she confessed. Her knees were wobbly and she sank down in the far corner of the sofa.

'Don't know! Weren't you supposed to be joining his business? Hadn't you discussed the ins and outs of the operation?'

Her pulse fluctuated in alarm. 'Try to understand. He was an old man, and he regarded me as a child. He wouldn't accept that I'd grown up and was capable of filling a useful place in society.' She wafted a dismissive hand. 'Oh yes, he'd spoken of me joining him in business, but I suspect he was just stringing me along. To Charlie I was a little girl. At heart he didn't want me to go out to work and possibly grow away from him.'

Drew glared at her. 'So in reality you haven't a clue how he amassed his fortune?'

Dismay halted her breath and she shook her head as the horrific implications bubbled through.

'You never asked any pertinent questions?' he demanded.

Nicole spread her palms. 'Why should I? As far back as I can remember he was buying and selling, perpetually on the phone to this man and that. It was a way of life I'd always known and accepted. I—I couldn't demand to see his balance sheets, could I?'

'So the money kept rolling in?' he said drily.

'Yes. On the rare occasions when I did ask questions he would laugh and say it would all be revealed in due time.'

'And?'

'It never was. He much preferred me to take an interest in pretty clothes, rather than stocks and shares.'

There was a soft breath of exasperation. 'Where did he base his business?'

The quagmire Nicole was struggling through thickened. 'There was an office in London, one room, but he was rarely there.'

'And your home, where was that?'

Nicole's stomach twisted. 'We had no fixed home as such. My mother and Charlie lived in various hotels, and I used to join them in the holidays from school and later, university.'

'Why the wanderlust?' Drew demanded.

It was too late for deception, now she must tell him the truth—in part.

'My mother, she—she loved the social scene, the bright lights. She enjoyed meeting new people, and after a few months she would develop itchy feet and need to be off again.'

She kept her eyes averted. There was no reason to draw his contempt by revealing the unsavoury details—that it was new men her mother itched to meet.

Drew shook his head in slow protest. 'Doesn't it seem more likely that Charles Werner could have kept on the move to avoid the tax man? No one in their right mind would want to live like that without a damn good reason. You say he dealt in commodities—that's a pretty loose description, it could mean anything. Sounds to me as though he was a wheeler-dealer.'

The unkind term cut her to the quick.

'I loved him,' she burst out emotionally. 'I don't care what you say. You never knew him, but he was a kind and decent person, and—and he cared about me.'

'I'm sure he did,' he agreed, rubbing a reflective hand across his jaw. 'Doubtless he wanted to provide you with the best things in life, no matter where the money came from.' He grimaced. 'In those kinds of transactions the law sometimes gets bent a little, but one thing is for certain, so far as the Tenerife debts are concerned, it was downright broken!'

Nicole's mind flew back to his original accusation. 'And you say *I* owe your company three thousand pounds?'

'Seems like it.'

Panic seized her. 'But I don't have three thousand pounds!'

'Then you'll have to raise it, won't you?' he drawled, with an indifferent shrug.

'How?'

'Use your imagination. Sell a few family hierlooms— that solitaire you're wearing must be worth a tidy sum.'

Her fingers flew upwards, protecting the stone from his gaze. 'This is mine,' she said doggedly. 'It was a twenty-first birthday present.'

Drew arched a sardonic brow. 'From Werner?'

'Yes.' Proud defiance angled her chin. 'And I'm certain there's no law which would force me to sell a gift given and received in good faith years ago.'

'Perhaps not, but it's morals we're discussing here. You know as well as I do that it's morally wrong for you to be living in the lap of luxury while some poor victim in Tenerife is on the breadline because your stepfather neglected to pay his bills.'

'I'm *not* living in the lap of luxury!'

Drew stretched up his arm languidly. 'Come on, Nicole, you might not class it as high living, but I assure you the majority of the world's population would beg to differ. You own a house in the country, an apartment in town, and you're a girl in your twenties who has never worked. For heaven's sake, many people slog out a lifetime and never possess one single brick of their own!'

She opened her mouth to protest and set the record straight, but he allowed her no access into his diatribe.

'Don't bother to justify yourself. The fact is that Charles Werner's money should be used to settle Charles Werner's debts.'

The conversation was moving out of reach, like a smoke-ring.

'What—what do you want me to do?' she stammered.

Drew sighed. 'We'll leave if for now.'

Nicole was weak with incredulity at the anti-climax. 'Leave it?' she echoed. He had locked her in a steel vault and then, without warning, flung wide the door to offer her freedom, albeit on a short chain.

'I only have details of the Benedict debt, not the others,' he explained. 'I've asked for further enquiries to be made.' He smiled and the switched-on charm bewildered her. 'Don't worry, everything will sort itself out.'

Her thoughts raced to review the previous summer. How hefty would the other debts be? There was the car, the doctor, a maidservant, groceries to be paid for—and what else?

Rising to his feet, Drew stretched out a hand to coax her up to join him. 'Don't look so distressed, poppet. These things happen all the time.'

He had shrugged off the mantle of judge and jury, abruptly becoming a friend, but Nicole was uneasy. What role would Drew choose to play next?

She assembled a measure of poise. 'I would never have applied for a position with your company if I'd been aware that Charlie owed you money,' she pointed out.

'I imagine not, though as they say in Yorkshire, "there's nowt so queer as folk." I must confess that if you hadn't mentioned Tenerife last night I would never have made any connection. Smith doesn't tie in with Werner, does it? Mind you, I did wonder if the Piña Coladas had loosened your tongue unwittingly.' He grinned at her look of consternation. 'I'm only joking, they weren't that potent.' He slid his hands around the supple curve of her waist. 'I'm sorry I had to come on strong, but I must protect my interests.'

His fingers had tightened, pulling her against him until the hard contact of his body made it impossible to deny the slow-fuse burn of attraction between them.

'Your interests?' Nicole repeated in bewilderment. 'The company, you mean?'

'Not only the company, my personal interests.' He gave a crooked smile. 'Surely you've noticed the effect you have on me? All the heavy breathing and glazed expressions?'

'You're suffering from Florida fever, that's all,' she rejoined, striving for flippancy.

'If I am, we'll have to think of a cure.'

He lifted a hand to her chin, steering it with slow deliberation to meet his kiss. The intimate warmth of mouth-on-mouth convinced Nicole she was about to fall apart at the seams. Charlie's debts floated from her mind as she clung to Drew, arms creeping up around his neck, her breasts pressing into the thin silk of his shirt.

'Do you really need a cure?' she whispered as they broke for air. 'Isn't it better to let a fever take its own course? On the other hand, it could turn out to be something far more lethal.'

As a shadow crossed his face Nicole instinctively knew she had said the wrong thing. She had put into words the possibility that their friendship might deepen, and now she saw that Drew was not happy at such a prospect. He still held her, still ran his palms along her back, pressing her into him, still nibbled at her lips until they parted again—but everything had changed.

She drew back. 'Perhaps you'd better find yourself a lady doctor to wipe your brow,' she said pertly, and an imp in her head made her add, 'with an impeccable background.'

Drew went very still. 'Why? Do you consider backgrounds matter that much?'

Nicole's head throbbed at the spectre of her mother's scurrilous path through life. When she raised her eyes she saw Drew was waiting for an answer with the steady unwavering gaze of a man who was mentally making decisions, decisions which could depend on her reply. The atmosphere was tense. She could not joke her way out of this one.

'No,' she said decisively. 'I think everyone deserves to be judged on their own merits. I would never condemn anyone if they were unfortunate enough to have some skeletons in their cupboard.'

'True, but don't you agree that we're all products of our pasts in some way? It might not look it, but beneath the trappings of success I'm a rough diamond, whereas you——' He left the words unsaid, but his lips moved into a self-mocking smile. 'There aren't any Swiss finishing schools on my family's score sheet.'

Nicole wrinkled her brow, trying to detect either envy or condemnation. 'You're not apologising, are you?'

'I'm bloody not!' he shot back with a violent burst of energy, and then grinned. 'But equally I hope I'm not an inverted snob. The fact is that you and I had very different childhoods, and so our concept of life varies.'

Nicole experienced a rush of pique, but could not decide why. 'You think it's nobler to start life poor than rich?' she demanded tartly, her grey-green eyes cold as the North Sea.

He laughed and pulled her back into his arms. 'You're going all hoity-toity again,' he teased, rubbing his mouth across her brow.

Nicole tried to ignore the way her skin tingled at his caress, but it was impossible, and when he bent his head to kiss her again she quite forgot why she had been feeling uptight.

'Oh hell!' he muttered, after a moment of delicious desire. 'I must go.' He glanced at his watch. 'I'm due at a business dinner in Miami in less than an hour. Don't fret over Werner's debts—when I discover how much cash is involved, we'll work something out.' He grinned mischievously. 'I don't intend to spend my weekends flying out to visit you behind bars in some Spanish gaol, though you'd look sensational in one of those suits with arrows, designed by Yves St Laurent!'

Her eyes danced. 'With handcuffs crafted by Tiffanys?'

He answered her smile. 'Naturally.' With a deliberate effort he pushed himself from her. 'I shan't be around for a couple of days, I have a series of meetings arranged over on the west coast of Florida. There are some parcels of land for sale in Sarasota which sound interesting, they're on the beach, with excellent access and——'

'I thought you were here on holiday,' Nicole remonstrated. 'You need to relax.'

He turned to grab a final kiss. 'You sound like my mother—so stop it!'

'Yes, sir,' she agreed, with such phoney meekness that they both laughed.

When Drew reached the door, he paused. 'If you're intending to visit Disney World with Mr and Mrs Purdy during their stay, count me in.'

Her shapely brows arched in surprise. 'The conservative Drew Benedict is risking a visit to a funfair!' she teased.

He laughed, his teeth strong and white against the

dark of his tan. 'One of these days I'll show you exactly what this battered, middle-aged conservative is willing to risk.'

'Is that a threat or a promise?'

'It's a warning, poppet,' he said, and winked.

Mrs Purdy seemed to talk non-stop for the next forty-eight hours. Every item in the show villa reminded her of some incident from the past which needed to be recounted, every view sparked off a garbled tale told at top speed, interspersed with names the woman took for granted meant something, when they meant nothing. There was scarcely pause for breath between one garrulous recitation and the next, and Nicole learnt to pity 'darling Kevin' and 'Patricia, who's such a pet', who were permanent fixtures in Mrs Purdy's life, whereas she, thank goodness, was only temporary.

This plethora of conversation left little time for private thoughts, for unlike Mr Purdy, Nicole felt it politic to show more interest than a vague mumble every ten minutes. Valiantly she tried to make sense of the haywire tales and thus was too exhausted to do more than fall into bed when she was released at the end of the day.

The few spare moments she did have were split equally between speculations on Charlie and Drew. The more she considered Charlie's behaviour over his last years, the more she convinced herself he had had money troubles. The cash with which she had bought Honeysuckle Haven had been a lump sum on her twenty-second birthday, and she well remembered how excessive it had been, even for Charlie who would have gift-wrapped the moon and given it to her if he could have managed it. His explanation that by her having the money then, she would avoid death duties, and that there would be nothing for her, subsequently, in his will had seemed reasonable. She had taken his words at face value, but now she wondered if his business affairs had already been in difficulties, and he had been in the process of securing her future while he could. Perhaps she had accepted the money naïvely, but what reason had there been for her not to believe what he said? He was her father figure, a man in his seventies with a lifetime's financial expertise behind him. Blithely she had invested the sum, withdrawing it after his death. An alarm bell rang in her head. Had she acted illegally by accepting the money and then purchasing the cottage? Nicole made a mental note to consult a solicitor once she returned to London and discover exactly where she stood.

The birthday money had been Charlie's final extravagance. From then on his gifts had been modest—books, perfume, clothes, though she had not craved more. All she had ever asked of Charlie was his love, and she had had that. The expensive gestures of the past had been forgotten, though now they seemed not so much forgotten as beyond his scope.

And yet he had insisted on renting the villa and arranging the sports car—the car Roberto had loved. Nicole's blood ran cold as she recalled her casual acceptance of the vehicle as a right, for hadn't Charlie hired a car for her every summer since she had learned to drive at eighteen? And while she and Roberto had been cruising along in the sunshine, the old man must have been racked with worry, worry which no doubt hastened his death. All he had cared about that last summer had been *her* happiness . . .

It was true she had received no money in his will. After the cremation, attended only by herself, Charlie's elder brother, and a handful of faceless old men who appeared in response to the notice in the obituary column, she had contacted his solicitor. Their meeting had been brief.

'Mr Werner left a bequest to a favourite charity and

the remainder of his estate to his brother,' she had been told. No details had been offered and she had asked no questions. It had been none of her business. At the back of her mind she had imagined the sum to be thousands, but in all probability it had been far more modest.

Nicole sighed. Her understanding had come too late. Poor Charlie—he had had a raw deal from her mother and now she wished she had been blessed with more insight and had realised the strain he must have been under during the last years. She had taken so much for granted . . .

One thing was certain, there was no way she could take Drew for granted. He might exhibit all the signs of falling for her, but she sensed his reservations ran deep, far deeper than perhaps he had yet realised. Whether she, as her mother's daughter, fitted into his scheme of things, was doubtful.

There was no point in dwelling on the future, she decided, tucking her khaki military-style shirt into matching cotton trousers. A rapid brushing of her hair, a smudge of avocado eye-shadow, and she was ready. Mr and Mrs Purdy had declared a strong interest in Disney World earlier in their visit, and now it was all arranged.

Drew leant across from behind the steering wheel to open the door of the large white Oldsmobile parked beneath the hotel porch.

'Hello, poppet. Give me a kiss, I've missed you,' he said, grinning when she scanned hastily around to check they were not overlooked. 'It's quite safe, no sign of your clients yet.'

When she slipped into the seat beside him, he reached out to hold her tight, his mouth hard on hers, aggressive and demanding, rough with desire.

'Nicki, Nicki,' he breathed, 'I've missed you so damned much!'

But when two figures appeared at the side window he jumped back in alarm, and now it was Nicole's turn to grin.

'Good morning. I'm Drew Benedict,' he said, climbing out to greet Mr and Mrs Purdy, and she saw him mentally click his heels and stand to attention.

There was no opportunity to chat on the drive to Orlando, despite her seat beside him, for Mrs Purdy commandeered the entire conversation. It transpired she had a nephew christened Andrew, also tagged Drew for short. He was a 'dream of a boy' and most of the journey was a verbal documentary of his progress through school. Nicole lent half an ear, eyeing the citrus groves and tousle-headed palms nodding their heads in the sunshine, but all the while aware of Drew. From time to time he would allow his hand to brush against her thigh, or cast a sidelong glance from beneath his dark lashes, and as Mrs Purdy's gossip swirled around they embarked on an elaborate game of feigned lack of interest in each other which built up, creeping like a burning fuse to a keg of dynamite.

Mrs Purdy moved on to her delight with Key Benedict, the villas and, rather embarrassingly, to Nicole's friendly assistance. Drew's look of pleasure hugged her to him like an encircling arm, making her soft as marshmallow inside, and after that the woman's chatter did not seem so bad.

Once the car was parked they followed hordes of holidaymakers to board a monorail for the journey from the vast parking lot to the entrance of the Magic Kingdom. As soon as they passed through the turnstiles, the colourful exciting spectacle which was Disney World began. There were painted barrows selling popcorn and ice-cream, flower stalls and sideshows, while cartoon characters mingled with the crowds. Town Square, which they visited first, was a bustling plazza of olde-worlde shops and cafés.

'I know you and Mrs Purdy would prefer to explore alone, sir,' Drew said firmly as they stood before the authentic City Hall. The silent Mr Purdy seemed to entertain a moment of doubt, but was allowed no chance to demur, for Drew swept on. 'I suggest we meet up again here, say at five o'clock.' He glanced over his shoulder at the Railroad Station where an old-fashioned steam train was setting out along the track, its whistle hooting merrily.

'You disposed of my clients with ruthless finality,' Nicole teased, as the older couple disappeared. 'But I'm supposed to be on duty—with them!'

His arm curved around her waist as they strolled through the attractive square with its gabled buildings and gardens bright with flowers.

'You *are* on duty,' he smiled. 'You're keeping the boss happy, and that's more important. Besides, that woman's chattering was sending me bananas, and I want to be alone with you.'

'Alone!' Nicole chuckled. Disney World was full of people. It resembled a giant film set where nothing seemed quite real, everything was larger than life. She smiled as a horse-drawn trolley car rumbled past.

'Not physically alone,' he concurred, swerving them into Main Street, which was lined with turreted turn-of-the-century shops and houses. 'But no one knows us here, so mentally it's just you and me.'

She grinned up at him. 'And you can relax!'

'Yes, madam.'

They sauntered along, pausing to admire goods in the shop windows or watch glass-blowing and demonstrations of other crafts. Everything was clean and brightly painted. People were laughing as they surged in and out of the souvenir shops, the candy stores, the penny arcades. Children were having their photographs taken with a life-size Minnie Mouse, and as they stopped to watch the fun she darted a glance at him. He *was* relaxed, tall and virile in a casual stud-fastened fawn shirt and denims, the warm breeze flicking strands of dark hair across his forehead.

Sensing her inspection, he smiled down, his hand firming at her waist, and the emotion she saw in his eyes made her heart race—for surely it was love? How could he say so much without words? His yearning was revealed in the blue eyes that wandered her face like a caress. Don't do this, Drew, she implored silently. Don't push us into something we'll both regret. She was drowning in the warmth of his smile, and when he pulled her close to kiss her brow she found herself snuggling against him. For a moment it seemed to be where she belonged, safe in the bend of his arm, but then she straightened. If she allowed herself to fall in love with him she was lining up more hurt, more pain, possibly more rejection. It was far safer to take their relationship slowly, to hold back until she had had time to explain the unpleasant facts of her background, and hope he would understand.

'Where shall we go first?' She turned the pages of the guide book in rapid succession. 'Adventure Land or Fantasy Land, or——'

He grinned, amused by her brisk change of mood. 'I'm yours to command, poppet,' he said, flashing a roguish smile. 'Whatever you want to do, I want to do.'

Nicole avoided his eyes, the sensual undercurrent was too strong, and instead she devoted her attention to a study of the map of the one-hundred-acre Magic Kingdom. 'Adventure Land first,' she pronounced.

'Pirates of the Caribbean' was their first stop—a dark sail through treasure troves and pirate strongholds where guns exploded around their ears and a rowdy crew of cocked-hat buccaneers called and leered at them from a rocking galleon. The highly sophisticated show was full of surprises which had them laughing delightedly, and they were still smiling when they moved on to see the Enchanted Tiki Birds. This was a musical revue where tropical birds and flowers, and even the pagan carvings on the doors, opened their mouths and sang with gusto. An out-of-doors jungle cruise in an explorer's launch was their final excursion before lunch, and as they sailed along the river surprisingly realistic 'wild' hippopotamuses and elephants appeared to bay and trumpet in the shallows, while dark-skinned tribes chanted war cries from the banks.

'It's amazing,' Drew agreed when they found a table in a cool, quiet restaurant lavishly decorated with potted palms and hanging baskets of greenery. He unloaded crisp salads and slices of Key Lime pie from the tray and sat down beside her. 'I don't know quite what I imagined Disney World to be, but it's a thousand times better.'

'So you don't mind if clients ask to come here?'

He chuckled, biting into a pink prawn. 'Not at all. I reckon if the villas don't entice them to Florida, then this place will.'

'It is the world's single most popular tourist attraction,' she pointed out. 'Fourteen million people come here to enjoy themselves every year.'

Drew raised thick brows. 'Okay, I'm converted, you don't need to quote your facts and figures. The only figure of interest right now is sitting beside me.'

The afternoon sped by as they visited one attraction after another, only stopping to grab a refreshing Coke and ice-creams. Five o'clock came much too soon and still they had not seen all of Disney World.

'We'll come for a second visit, some time,' Drew decided as they met up with Mr and Mrs Purdy.

The drive back to Key Benedict was a repeat performance of the morning, with Mrs Purdy in full flow now, armed with the day's fresh stimulation. Within minutes everyone else lapsed into silence and even Nicole followed Mr Purdy's example, resorting to a vague 'Uh-huh' now and then.

She felt the cool strength of Drew's fingers on her wrist holding her back as the other couple climbed from the car at the end of the journey. With a weary smile from Mr Purdy and a high-powered concerto of thanks and goodbyes from his wife, they departed.

Drew gave his head a little shake. 'I'm shell-shocked after that!'

'She is hard going,' Nicole agreed.

'Hard going! You deserve danger money for coping with her, and how that poor bloke survives I've no idea. I thought my mother was a gossip, but she's as talkative as the Mona Lisa compared with that one.' He strummed the back of her hand with his fingers. 'Have dinner with me, Nicki?'

'Yes, please, but can we go somewhere away from Key Benedict?'

Nicole was hedging her bets. By keeping their friendship under wraps it would be less traumatic if, or when, they broke up. Rochelle, Jean and José were bound to expect some kind of explanation if she and Drew were close one minute and distant the next.

'Why?' he asked, narrowing his eyes.

She flipped a careless hand. 'Just for a change.'

'Okay. I must go down to the office now to check on a few things. Suppose I collect you around nine?' She nodded in agreement. 'We'll eat,' Drew continued, 'and then we'll come back to the villa and——'

The flow of energy between their eyes was electric, and a ripple of desire travelled from Nicole's head to her toes. 'Let's not move too fast, Drew,' she said with a shaky smile. Her limbs had turned to water and it was an effort to push at the car door.

Turning, he caught her jaw in his fingers, holding her close. 'I can't help it,' he said simply.

After a leisurely shower and shampoo, Nicole dressed. She had plenty of time, and the tranquillity of her room had a soporific effect after the hot bustle of the day. Humming to herself, she blow-dried her hair, flicking it back from her face and paying special attention to the silky fringe. She chose harem-style trousers and a matching camisole top in azure-blue georgette, fastened at the waist with a wide gold belt. She made up her face with care, silver-gold eye-shadow with lashings of sooty mascara and a slick of pearly lip-gloss. Following fashion, she knotted a fine golden band under her hair and across her brow, then stood back to examine the reflection in the mirror. Nicole tried to see herself as Drew saw her. Did she drip affluence? Did years of the rich life make her different from her less pampered contemporaries? The harem suit was Paris-designed but had been bought three years ago. Surely she looked just like any smart modern girl out on a date? She caught her lower lip between sharp white teeth. She was what she was, and the sooner she explained to Drew exactly what that encompassed, the better.

As she was applying a final coat of nail polish an abrupt staccato at the door made her jump. Her wristwatch revealed that it was only half-past eight, too early for Drew. Carefully she lifted the latch to avoid damaging her wet nails, then stepped back in surprise. It *was* Drew, though surely he had not arrived to take her out, because he was still wearing the casual shirt and blue jeans.

'Hello.' Nicole's radiant smile, so generously offered, froze midway between pleasure and apprehension, for his features were grim.

He strode into the living-room, swivelling as she joined him. A mix of emotions flickered across his face like images on a screen and Nicole waited, trapped in a time warp as anxiety began crawling over her.

'It's Charlie, isn't it? You've discovered that the other

debts are sky-high?' She was panic-striken.

Drew ran a hand through his over-long hair. 'No,' he rasped. 'They only come to around a thousand.'

'A thousand!' she squeaked. 'A thousand pounds is a lot of money.'

Mindlessly she was wafting her hands to dry off the varnish.

'Cut it out, Nicole. Quit acting the pauper! A thousand pounds means nothing to you. You must have wheedled a hell of a sight more than that out of Charles Werner, but you picked the wrong man when you took me for a sucker!'

'You?' Her eyes stretched wide. 'What are you talking about?'

Drew stuck his hands into his pockets. His lips were jammed together and he examined his feet for a tense moment, then his head whipped up and challenging metallic blue eyes pierced hers.

'I'm talking about the subtle whoring that you indulge in. The way women like you move from one rich man to the next.' A nerve throbbed unevenly in his temple. 'What were you going to do? Get me into bed and then coax me into paying your debts, or perhaps I should say Charles Werner's debts, as you insist you know nothing about them.' He gave a dry bark of derision. 'No way, Nicole. I don't buy my sex, however beautifully it's packaged.'

She stared at him, unable to believe her ears.

'You bastard!' she spat in outrage.

'If anyone's a bastard around here, madam, it's far more likely to be you,' he sneered. 'Charles Werner was not your father, or your stepfather. He was no damned relation at all. The only tie between you and him was cash—cold hard cash.'

The words were bullets, he was firing them through her brain.

Drew rested his weight on one foot and folded his

arms. 'Come on, Nicole,' he taunted, his eyes burning blue fire. 'Aren't you going to tell me about that cosy *ménage à trois* you enjoyed—mother, daughter and rich old man?'

She swallowed hard, fighting the impulse to cower away from his insulting tone.

'I was going to explain, Drew, but—but everything has happened so quickly. It's true Charlie wasn't my father, but I—I always regarded him as such.'

'Exactly,' he snarled, his lip curling. 'He was your sugar daddy!'

CHAPTER SIX

'*No!*' Her cry ripped across the room.

'You denied Werner's debts and they're a reality, so why bother to waste your breath this time?' Drew frowned. 'For the past hour I've been talking with our man in Tenerife, and he gave me all the facts. He's friendly with some guy who managed a hotel in St Lucia which your little trio graced with your presence, so they got together and——'

'And dished the dirt!' she said bitterly.

'No one knows about the dirt better than you,' he replied with deliberate insolence. 'My heavens, you and your mother must have fastened on to that poor old man like limpets! No doubt your mother snared him first and when you grew up, becoming prettier by the minute, you took over. How old were you when you offered yourself to him in return for cash, Nicole— fourteen, fifteen?'

She slapped his face hard, twice. Only the steely fingers that clamped around her wrists prevented her from striking him a third time.

'It wasn't like that at all,' she stormed, struggling for freedom, her breasts rising and falling in agitation, her hair swirling around her face.

'He supported the pair of you for twenty years,' Drew said icily, controlling her struggles with no visible effort. 'But being his mistress wasn't enough, was it? Behind Werner's back you took other lovers. It appears to have been one glorious procession of men. The hotels must have buzzed with gossip, because you sound to have had one hell of a reputation!'

'That wasn't me,' she sobbed, trying to wrench herself from his grip. She closed her eyes in despair. 'That was my—my mother.'

'Your mother!' A disdainful smile lifted one corner of his mouth. 'You don't expect me to believe that.'

His contempt was infuriating and she glowered up at him, deriving malicious satisfaction from the fiery imprint of her hand on his cheek. She would have hit him again if she could.

'I don't give a damn what you believe, but if your contact in Tenerife checks up he'll discover that Charles Werner's so-called mistress was in her fifties.'

'Isn't that a little old for having lovers?' he sneered. 'At fifty most women are more interested in grand-children and home baking.'

Despite her wriggles he refused to release his hold and Nicole had to bow to the inevitable—brute force reigned supreme. She fell still.

'Perhaps in your world,' she replied. 'But my mother wasn't a stereotype, being a housewife would have driven her crazy.' Head held high, she felt a spark of pride. 'She was sexy and beautiful. She looked nowhere near her true age and men flocked around her like moths around the proverbial flame.'

'Including Werner?' Drew said heavily.

'Charlie and my mother were not lovers. It was a platonic arrangement.'

'Oh yes?' he drawled in patent disbelief.

'Yes,' Nicole insisted, furious at the way he was effectively handcuffing her. She yanked back viciously to test his reaction, but the grip was relentless. 'Your information is all wrong, you've been misinformed.'

'Give me your version.'

'Let me go first,' she demanded. 'I won't be your prisoner!'

'Won't you? It seems to me you already are. I employ you. You're living in *my* hotel at *my* expense on *my* island, and it's *my* air ticket which will get you back to England. Should I decide to cancel that ticket you'll be trapped here. You're totally at my mercy, and you're in my debt.' He lifted a shoulder in a scornful shrug. 'Though I suppose you could always latch on to another patron. José is a soft touch, I should bear him in mind.' Abruptly he released her, deserting the cruel banter. 'Sit down. I want the truth, Nicole, and nothing but.'

She sat down, rubbing her wrists and refusing to be cowed by his stern aggression. Her jaw thrust forward belligerently. 'My mother had many lovers,' she began.

'And you followed suit?'

Nicole curled tight fingers into her palms. 'No.' She swallowed hard, forcing herself to keep on an even keel. 'My mother married twice and divorced twice in quick succession when she was young, then—she met my father. She told me that if he had lived she would have remained faithful to him. It's a cosy idea, but impossible to take seriously.' Her voice trailed off and she fidgeted with the wide gold belt at her waist. 'They were married one January, but the following summer my father was killed in a flying accident, and I arrived soon after Christmas. Certainly he was the only one she was prepared to have a child with, so perhaps she did care for him more than the rest.'

'And your father was called Smith?'

She flashed him a toxic glance. 'Steven Smith. You can check the birth, marriage and death certificates, it's all there. I'm quite legal!'

'Where does Charles Werner fit into this?'

Nicole studied her nails. 'After I was born my mother used the remnants of my father's money to finance a holiday in the Greek Islands. Staying at home washing baby clothes wasn't her scene, so she stuck me in a carry-cot and flew off into the sunshine. She wasn't alone for long. There was always some man willing to help with her luggage, or to pace up and down with me when I was teething.'

'She carted you around with her—and her men?'

A bleak smile flickered and died. 'Yes. Just because you're—not respectable it doesn't mean you don't love your child. She was a good enough mother in her way.'

'And Werner?' he prompted.

'Charlie was staying at the same hotel. He would have been around fifty at the time, and he was a confirmed bachelor on his own with not much in his life.'

'But rich,' he inserted drily.

'But rich,' she repeated with a sigh of exasperation. 'He loved babies and made a beeline for me. Apparently my mother dashed off with the young man of the moment and left him baby-sitting for days on end. Charlie loved it! Over the next four years their paths crossed, increasingly so because he made a point of discovering where my mother and I would be.'

'And your mother encouraged him?'

Nicole shook her head. 'Why should she? She had no difficulty in attracting virile young men who could maintain her lifestyle. The prospect of Charlie as her lover was laughable, he was far too respectable and staid. He didn't approve of her either as a woman or as a mother.' She paused. 'Her behaviour appalled him— over the years they had some furious battles. No, Charlie disliked my mother, but he was besotted with me. He begged her to allow him to adopt me, but she refused and so he—he insinuated himself into our lives.' Her eyes softened with remembered pleasure. 'When I was little he would arrive out of nowhere, and suddenly the world lit up. His pockets would be overflowing with sweets, he would play with me, tell me jokes, listen to my tales—all the things my mother never did.'

'She was too occupied with her boy-friends?' Drew was leaning against the kitchen bar, listening intently.

'Yes, she was grateful because Charlie took me off her hands. She knew she was the wrong influence for a child and saw the sense in Charlie's proposition.' Nicole licked dry lips. 'In return for him having control over my upbringing and education, he offered to support us. I believe my mother accepted because she wanted the best for me.'

'Heart-warming!'

His jeer made her grit her teeth, but she refused to retaliate. 'Okay, perhaps the money was part of it. No way could she afford to send me to boarding school. Her lovers might have been happy to finance her, but not a schoolgirl daughter as well.'

'Werner's offer must have been one no self-respecting whore could refuse.'

'Oh, but you're nasty!' she flared. 'My mother was thinking of me, too. It can't have been much fun having a critical old bachelor breathing down your neck all the time.'

'So you made up a threesome?'

'Yes, Charlie laid down the rules—that my mother was to be discreet.' Nicole tugged the golden band from her head and ran it between her fingers. 'Though of course she rarely was.' But he was attempting to provide respectability, a steadying hand for me, and, at heart, she respected that. She used to rant and rave about him being a fussy old bore, but——' Nicole shrugged, 'Charlie was a father by nature, though for some reason he had never married and I was the—the child of his old age.'

'He spent thousands on you—the child of a woman he neither respected nor liked—merely for the pleasure of watching you grow?'

Drew was nailing her to the sofa with the cold scorn in his eyes.

'Can't you understand, Charlie and I were each other's family!' she cried. 'It's all right for you, you have a stable background, but we were both adrift. We needed each other, the money was unimportant——'

'Unimportant!' He cut her short with a withering frown which, as a rule, silenced the opposition, but Nicole was beyond caring.

'Yes, unimportant!' she yelled. 'Okay, my mother revelled in a luxurious way of life. She needed fancy clothes to keep the men interested, but what mattered to me was Charlie's love, not his bank account. I didn't give a damn about the expensive schools, the birthday presents. All I wanted was his love, his constancy, to know he would always be there when I needed him and that had nothing to do with money.'

'But you didn't refuse any of it?'

It was a drawled statement of fact.

'You're so—so *mercenary*!' she snarled through clenched teeth, and the golden band between her fingers snapped. 'I was a baby when he came into my life, hardly old enough to work a pocket calculator to check if he could afford my expensive whims!' she sneered. 'Yes, I enjoyed the sweets and toys he provided—any child would—but I also liked to cuddle up on his knee when he told me stories, and run to him for comfort when I grazed my knees. It was Charlie who tucked me up in bed at night, Charlie who encouraged me and reprimanded me when I was a teenager.'

'And it was Charlie who left behind debts of four thousand pounds in Tenerife,' Drew interrupted.

'*Yes*!' she slammed back.

He stuck his thumbs into the belt-loops on his jeans. 'Then I rest my case.'

'What case?' Nicole was yelling, her cheeks pink with fury, her hair tumbling across her brow. 'He was a sick old man——'

'He was a criminal!'

'The only reason he must have allowed the bills to mount and then got away quickly was to indulge *me*.'

'Precisely.'

The pain in her heart was threatening to choke her.

'And you think that makes him my—my sugar daddy?' she managed to ask.

Drew shrugged, circling a pattern on the carpet with the toe of his sports shoe. 'Perhaps you didn't sleep with him——'

'You're damn right I didn't!'

'But it's still an odd set-up. I'll have to think about it.'

His lukewarm response annoyed her intensely.

'Will you! Can't your petty suburban mind grasp that there are people who don't fit into neat little slots?' Nicole tossed her head defiantly. 'And who the hell are you to judge me? Perhaps your contact in Tenerife also told you about my red-hot affair last summer with Roberto Rodriguez? You surely can't believe one man in his seventies was sufficient to keep me satisfied? After all, rich bitches can have their pick, can't they? You must have realised I have morals like an alleycat.' There was a sob in her voice and when she raised her fingers to her face she discovered she was crying, scalding tears pouring down her cheeks. 'Roberto was a handsome Spaniard. He used to take me to the beach, driving the sports car Charlie never paid for, and kiss me and——'

'Stop it!' Drew thundered. He grabbed hold of her shoulders and yanked her to her feet. 'Stop it,' he said a second time, but his voice was choked and he was trembling. Then he was shaking her and holding her, and she was sobbing against his shoulder as though her heart would burst.

'Nicki, Nicki, don't cry,' he pleaded. 'I believe you.'

With a gulp she brushed the tears from her eyes and stepped from him, shuddering with emotion. 'I want to resign from your company.'

'No, there's no need for that,' he said, offering a handkerchief.

'Isn't there? Aren't you afraid I might try to seduce one of your clients now that you're not going to fall into my hands like a solid gold apple?'

'Finish this spell in Florida and we'll discuss things when you go back to London,' he suggested.

Nicole wiped away her tears. 'There's nothing to discuss. I'll work out a month's notice here, I believe that is in my contract, and in the meantime you can train some other girl.' She returned the handkerchief. 'Would you go now, please.'

'Nicki!'

A hand rested on her shoulder, but she shrugged herself free.

'I can't pay back your three thousand pounds immediately. The best I can do is give you my word that I'll raise the money within six months. If that isn't good enough and you prefer to take me to court, that's your prerogative. As you said, Drew, I'm at your mercy.'

She walked forward and held wide the door, waiting for him to leave.

'Stay with the company,' he said. 'I'm sure you can sell the villas.'

'I'm sure I can, but not within the next four weeks. I'm sorry I shan't be around to see them all occupied. They're beautiful properties, I'd like to own one myself.' She fixed him with scathing eyes. 'But a girl like me would, wouldn't she?'

Despite the illuminated 'seat-belts on' sign and the stewardess's request that 'everyone remain seated until the plane comes to a complete standstill', the old lady beside Nicole insisted on standing on tiptoe to search in the overhead locker. The plane lurched on its path along the runway, the old lady swayed, and an assortment of coats, rugs and packages cascaded into the aisle. Up rushed the stewardess, scolding loudly, while the old lady and other passengers disentangled themselves from the debris.

Smothering a smile, Nicole turned to gaze out of the porthole at the airport buildings, remembering her departure six weeks ago. Then Sir William and Lady Whitman had been with her; everyone had been in high spirits and the future had seemed rosy. But now . . .

Drew, it seemed, had walked out of her room and out of her life that dreadful evening. José reported that the boss had decided to cut short his visit and return to London the very next day. She knew it made sense to be grateful he had gone—there could be no further accusations now—but, perversely, she had missed him. Nicole bit deep into her lip. Of the two men she had cared for, the first had left because he considered her too poor, while the other—what *did* Drew think of her? That she was a scheming parasite, willing to sell herself body and soul for the price of a pampered existence? No, he had said he believed her version of the facts. In any case he would have checked and discovered her mother had been the notorious butterfly. But, like it or not, she was still her mother's daughter and could not blame Drew if he harboured some doubts. And then there were Charlie's debts . . .

She squared her shoulders beneath the zipped honey-coloured flying suit. Honeysuckle Haven would be put on the market at a cheap enough price to ensure a prompt sale. Recouping her original outlay would be impossible and the money spent on repairs and renovations would be forfeited, but that was unfortunate. Cash in hand was what she required—and fast. Once the Benedict debt, and the others, were cleared she could hold her head up again, but until then . . .

When she reached the baggage carousel all the trolleys had been taken and Nicole struggled through Customs with her two leather suitcases and bulging bags, heartily wishing she had learned the art of travelling with only a spare pair of panties and a toothbrush.

'I'll carry those,' a deep voice informed her as she emerged on to the concourse.

Raising her head, she froze motionless, clinging on to her suitcases for dear life. Drew stood before her, a lean figure in a burgundy leather jacket and matching cords.

He gave a lopsided grin. 'You seem to be weighed down.'

'I can manage perfectly well on my own, thank you,' she told him, and promptly had to lurch forward to catch her travel bag before it thudded on to the floor.

'I'm the one with the muscles, poppet,' he said, full of smug masculine amusement as he commandeered the suitcases, then his brows pulled together. 'What the hell have you got in here—gold bars?'

Nicole glared at him. 'Naturally. I met this geriatric in a wheelchair on the beach at Miami and——'

'And you showed him your spectacular suntan and fell heir to a fortune?' he continued, grinning broadly.

'How did you guess?' she snapped.

He carried on grinning, immune to her frosty hauteur.

'I suppose you checked the facts about my background?' she demanded, her high heels rapping as she walked along beside him.

'Yep.'

'And now you want to apologise?'

Drew glanced at the frosty profile. 'Yep.'

He said no more, his strides lengthening until it was all she could do to keep pace.

'Well?' she panted, as they reached a flight of steps.

'I apologise.'

Drew was bounding up, two at a time despite having a suitcase in each hand, and when she caught up with him at the top she took a deep breath and asked, 'Is that it?'

'Yep.'

'Rochelle was right, you *are* a male chauvinist pig!'

'Yep.'

Her temper was starting to get the better of her.

'Is that all you have to say?'

'No. I've missed you.'

'I bet!'

Now it was her turn at brevity, for the sincerity in his words made her pulses leap so erratically that she had no strength left for more. He had missed her!

'Cross my heart and hope to die,' he assured her. 'I've spent all my nights wondering if I should invest in binoculars and fly over to Florida for some birdwatching.'

He paused to study the overhead signs, then swung left following the arrows to the car park. Nicole had no alternative but to follow.

'And what stopped you?' she asked, lightheaded with a happiness she was careful to conceal.

Drew pulled down the corners of his mouth in self-mockery. 'My mother! When I flew back here she declared I looked like death warmed up and made me go to the doctors. I had all sorts of tests.'

'What was the problem?' she asked, eyes stretched with sudden worry.

'Florida fever,' he replied, deadpan. 'So it was no work, no cigars, no flying for three weeks.' The furrow beside his mouth took shape. 'But I still need plenty of t.l.c.'

'Tender loving care?'

'Tanned luscious curves, preferably wrapped around me very tightly.'

There was unholy glee in the blue eyes that met hers, and Nicole had to smile.

'That's better,' he said. 'I don't like it when you go all hoity-toity on me.'

A group of Indian travellers appeared ahead, the women vivid in floating saris of purple and cerise, and their progress was forced to a halt. By the time the way was clear Nicole had straightened out her expression and her thoughts. Even if Drew had missed her, he was still the man who changed his women every five minutes. The only reason he might want to hold on to her a little longer would be to ensure she repaid Charlie's debt. She put a restraining hand on his arm.

'I'm grateful for your help with my suitcases, but I'll make my own way to the Underground, thank you.'

'You don't imagine I came all the way out here first thing on a Saturday morning merely to act as porter, do you?' he asked, ignoring the sign for the Underground and instead making for a distant door.

'I have no idea why you came,' she replied, and then frowned. 'How did you know the flight I would take?'

'I telexed José and told him I wanted to meet you.'

For a moment Nicole swung between pleasure at his desire to see her again, and irritation at his blithe interference in her affairs. Irritation won.

'Won't he think it odd, or do you make a habit of meeting all your returning employees, Mr Benedict?' she taunted scathingly.

'Only those who are young and pretty—and who owe me four thousand pounds!'

The answer was corrosive, bitten out. No longer was Drew cajoling, and icy fingers scampered along her spine at his change of mood. Too late, she wished she had been pleasanter. He had come as a friend, but her snapping had put a stop to all that.

'*Four* thousand?' she echoed faintly.

'I arranged for the other debts in Tenerife to be settled. It was done discreetly, the police were informed that the money came from Charles Werner's estate. No awkward questions were asked.'

'Thank you,' Nicole mumbled.

Drew steered her out between sliding glass doors into the open air.

'Why thank me? It's your money. Instead of paying me three thousand pounds, now you pay four.'

'I'll settle the debt as soon as possible,' she promised when they arrived at the gleaming Jaguar.

Drew stacked her luggage in the boot and lowered himself into the car, waiting as she sat beside him.

'How do you propose to raise the cash?' He glanced at the diamond hanging in the open vee of her flying suit. 'Even that beauty won't have a resale value of four thousand pounds.'

'I'll never sell this, never!' she declared, fingering the solitaire.

'You can't have your cake and eat it. The money must be raised somehow,' he said flatly. 'You can't cling on to your assets forever.'

'I know that,' she returned crisply. 'I'm arranging to sell my cottage. I intend going out there this afternoon.'

Leaving the car park, Drew swung out on to the road signposted for the motorway.

'Do you need to actually sell?' he asked, giving her a sharp glance. 'You only owe four thousand——'

'Only!' she interspersed, but he ignored her.

'Do you own the cottage outright?'

She nodded.

'Then a bank will lend you money against it. Property is one of the most worthwhile investments there is. Don't dispose of your cottage just to raise such a small sum.'

They had reached the motorway, and as Drew accelerated into the fast lane, Nicole frowned, wondering why he appeared to be helping her. But he was not helping *her*, was he? He was making damned certain she repaid the debt.

'It's best if I sell,' she said determinedly. 'The cottage was a—a bad buy. I've left myself very tight on cash, there's not much sense——'

'There's not much sense in a single girl loading herself up with a cottage *and* an apartment if she's short of money,' Drew cut in. 'I bet the rates on your city apartment are mind-boggling—I know mine are.' He scowled at her. 'What's your annual outlay?'

In dismay she visualised the paltry bedsit. 'I—I don't know,' she gabbled. 'Look, please could you drop me off when we reach Oxford Street? I have some shopping to do.'

'Shopping, with those two suitcases? Don't be foolish. I'll run you home.'

'No!' It came out as a squawk of terror.

'Why not? What's wrong?'

Nicole swallowed, heartily wishing she had kept to Charlie's dictum of no lies. 'I don't own an apartment,' she confessed, flushing scarlet. 'I just rent a bedsit.'

'Huh!' Drew took his eyes off the road for a moment to flash her a glance. 'And the cottage, is that a figment of your imagination, too?'

'No, no, it's real,' she assured him. 'It's mine, I do own it.'

'How do I know you're telling me the truth?'

'You don't, you'll just have to trust me.'

She risked a covert glance at his expression—it was grim, and when he spoke his voice was equally so.

'But I have no reason to trust you, Nicole. For all I know you could be a hustler.' He didn't need to add, 'Just like your mother,' it was written all over his darkly brooding face.

There was a hard pain in her chest. When Drew had met her he had been content to wipe the slate clean and start afresh in friendship, but her pigheaded attitude had changed all that, and now her deceit over the bedsit had revived his doubts about her. It was as though the unsavoury facets of her life were scrawled in his mind like obscene graffiti.

There was nothing more to say and for the remainder of the journey she sat mute, only breaking the taut silence to give directions. As the suburbs grew shabbier and shabbier Drew's jaw tightened and when, finally, they pulled to a halt at the kerbside, he wound down his window and stared in horror.

'You can't live there!' he exclaimed, frowning at the peeling paintwork, the dingy curtains.

Instantly Nicole was on the defensive. 'It's cheap to rent.'

'It looks it!'

Choosing to ignore the acerbic comment, she climbed from the car, her brow puckering as a group of raggle-taggle children clustered around to watch Drew lift her luggage on to the pavement. They were eyeing the Jaguar with interest, and she remembered how windscreen wipers, tyres and even engines have been reputed to disappear from unattended vehicles in five minutes flat.

'Thanks for the lift,' she said. 'I'll be in touch about the money as soon as possible. Goodbye.'

Drew locked the car. 'Oh no, I'm coming into this joint to take a look, and from the condition of the outside it promises to be something of a culture shock.' Observing the whispering children, he zipped open the leather jacket and produced his wallet. 'Who's the leader of the gang?' he asked.

A tall negro boy of about thirteen, wearing a red knitted hat, stepped forward. 'Me, mister.'

Drew peeled off a pound note. 'This is for now, and if you make sure there's not so much as a fingerprint on my car when I return, you'll get more. Understand?'

'Yes, mister. Thanks, mister,' the boy smiled, his teeth shining white in his face.

Nicole's landlady's eyes nearly popped out of their sockets when she answered Drew's knock, and with a coy smile she shuffled off ahead of them up the stairs, spattering cigarette ash and commenting on the weather with unusual affability. Nicole noted that it was acceptable to be well dressed if you were male, and good-looking with it!

'Home sweet home,' she announced defiantly when

the woman managed to tear herself from Drew's blue eyes. There was the sound of coughing as she slapped away down the stairs in her slippers.

It needed only three of his strides to cross the room. He ran a discerning finger along the window ledge, frowned at the gas ring and cracked sink, clicked his tongue over a wobbly electric fitting, and then tested the narrow bed which creaked alarmingly beneath his weight. 'The Ritz it isn't,' he commented.

'*I'm* not complaining.'

He scrubbed across his moustache with a thoughtful thumb, his eyes grave, then sat down again on the bed. Watching him, Nicole realised the room had shrunk, or was it Drew's six foot three inches which made it seem like a cubicle? Even the bed appeared smaller, and she had a comical image of him sleeping in it, feet sticking out at the end, arms hanging over the sides.

'Okay, let's go,' he ordered, and the image faded. There was no way he would ever sleep in *her* bed! 'We'll grab something to eat and then I'll run you out to that cottage of yours.'

It was tempting to avoid the long bus ride and subsequent trek to Honeysuckle Haven, for although Nicole had slept on the overnight flight from Miami, it had been a shallow sleep and only the nervous rush of adrenaline Drew was promoting had kept her alert. But Drew was alert, too. He would inspect the cottage as critically as he had inspected her room.

'No, thank you.'

'Oh yes, madam,' he replied, allowing no room for disagreement. 'You could skip out of here any time and I'd never be able to trace you. I want to see that cottage of yours, I want to see where *my* money is invested.' He tossed a sneering glance around her shabby quarters. 'There's nothing here that could raise four pounds, let alone four thousand.'

Drew's protection money had paid off. The Negro boy was strutting between the car and the wide-eyed gang of children, fists clenched at the ready, and it was obvious from his swagger that no one had been foolish enough to chance their luck.

'Didn't even let 'em breathe on it,' he announced, hurling a supercilious look at his audience. To his great delight Drew produced the promised payment, and they drove off to a chorus of, 'Let me look after your car next time, mister' and 'I'll clean it for you, too!'

Nicole had not realised she was hungry, but when they were installed in a booth at a Knightsbridge restaurant the brunch menu looked appetising, and she found herself duplicating Drew's order of bacon, egg and tomatoes, followed by toast and piping hot coffee.

As they ate she decided that, for the moment, there was nothing to be gained by fighting him every inch of the way. Now that she had worked out her notice he was no longer her employer, but she did owe him the money, and that allowed him some rights.

Drew had abandoned his attacking position, and the meal passed pleasantly, rather to her surprise, as they talked about this and that.

'You'd please my mother,' he told her with a grin. 'She's always rabbiting on about how much she likes people who enjoy their food.'

Nicole eyed her empty plate with embarrassment as it dawned on her that she had wolfed everything down in about five minutes flat. 'It was delicious,' she defended. 'I'm back to home cooking now and, to be honest, it's not one of my strong points.'

'Didn't they teach you Cordon Bleu at that finishing school?'

She took a sip of coffee, wrapping her hands around the cup. 'They did, but I only possess one temperamental gas ring, and in any case most of the recipes call for gallons of fresh cream, or smoked salmon, or pheasant, so——'

Drew arched a dark brow. 'So?'

'So I whip round the corner and buy myself fish and chips, or a packet of crisps instead.'

Drew reached into the inside pocket of his jacket and produced an envelope. 'Here you are,' he said, handing it to her. 'You'll be able to treat yourself to *two* packets of crisps now.'

Suspiciously Nicole pulled out the flap.

'It's your salary,' he explained. 'I thought you might prefer cash, rather than suffer the delay of it passing through your bank account.'

She felt a stab of chagrin at his intuition. It was as though he knew that all she possessed right now was the few pounds she had changed back from the dollars he had lent her. One of the reasons for visiting Honeysuckle Haven that afternoon was to collect the rent.

'Incidentally,' he continued, 'I hope you don't mind, but I decided to repay Rochelle for the contact lenses.'

Nicole's head snapped up. 'Why? Didn't you believe I would honour my debt?' she demanded bitterly, the grey-green eyes burning with sudden resentment.

He reached across the table and covered her hand with his. 'Calm down!' His fingers were firm, refuting her gesture for freedom. 'It's easier, that's all. It saves changing your pounds back into dollars.'

'So now I owe *you* the price of the lenses. What are you, Drew, some kind of clearing house for all my debts?' She heard the bleak intonation in her voice and knew she was being unfair.

Releasing her hand, he snapped his fingers for the waiter. Some lunatic in her head suggested she demand that he add the cost of the meal on to her burgeoning debit account, but at the last moment she decided not to risk his anger. The taut dark face was indication enough that Drew could erupt, given the slightest provocation.

As Nicole rose from the table remorse seeped into her. She had rejected his help unkindly, but she was weary, she justified. Nine hours flying across the Atlantic was a long time, and now he was trampling all over her when she could manage nicely on her own, thank you. But could she? And, more to the point, did she want to?

'I'm sorry I was ungrateful,' she apologised when they were back in the car, and rested her head against his shoulder in a quest for reassurance.

For a moment Drew remained aloof then, with a sigh of half amused exasperation, he turned to her. 'You're tired, poppet. Give me the directions to the cottage and then try to sleep.'

She did as she was told, giving Drew much entertainment as she carefully removed her contact lenses. When they were deposited in their plastic case, she sank into her seat and within minutes was fast asleep.

The lack of motion woke her. She rubbed her eyes, starting the lazy swim to the surface through waves of sleep, while Drew watched on, his face grave, wearing the same look he had worn at Disney World—the look of love.

As she focussed, she went very still inside. Drew, she said silently, when you look at me like that I think you love me, and I think I love you, too. Her heart stopped beating. I *know* I love you. Now she realised why all the determined nights out with José, Rochelle and Jean, all the parties, the discos, the laughter, had failed to satisfy her. It was Drew she needed to make her life whole, though—heaven knew—he couldn't need her . . .

Briskly she replaced her lenses and combed her hair. When she was ready, Drew climbed from the car, removing his leather jacket to reveal a wine-coloured sports shirt. He eyed the cottage and stretched his long arms lazily above his head.

'This is vastly different from your—apartment!' he teased, with an approving glance at Honeysuckle Haven.

Bathed in summer sunshine, the cottage was at its best, and Nicole flushed with pride until she considered the problems its acquisition had caused, and then her face fell. But Drew looked impressed, and as they walked up the path he acquired the air of a shrewd property magnate, his eyes assessing the thatched roof, the latticed windows, the rough white walls. She rang the bell and as they waited he fingered the creamy-white blossoms of honeysuckle which trailed luxuriously across the porch.

'Mmm,' he said, sniffing extravagantly at its fragrance. 'Smells nearly as good as you.'

His compliment went unanswered because Mrs Foster opened the door at that very moment. Nicole wondered why she had bothered to comb her hair in the car, for she received only a cursory glance before the middle-aged woman gave her full attention to Drew, who appeared to have to do nothing more than exist to hold centre stage. Mrs Foster was unable to take her eyes off him and it was apparent he would not be allowed to fade into the background as Nicole had wished.

'May I introduce Mr Benedict,' she said as they were ushered into the living-room, for introductions could not be avoided in the light of her tenant's interest in him. 'He's—he's my——'

She dried up. What exact capacity did Drew fill? Overlord? Creditor? Bailiff? One thing was certain, his inspection of the oak beams that punctuated the ceiling revealed he was far more than a disinterested friend.

'Fiancé,' he said calmly into the silence.

Mouth agape, she stared at him.

'Oh, I didn't know you were——' Mrs Foster began, turning to Nicole with a look of renewed respect.

'It was sudden,' he announced, striding to peer into the wide inglenook hearth. 'We're deciding what to do about this place when we're married—whether to hang on or put it on the market.' He smiled back over his shoulder. 'Naturally we'll give you plenty of time to find fresh accommodation.'

Mrs Foster proferred a flustered, 'Thank you.'

'Okay if I take a stroll around?' he asked, flashing a high-powered grin that had the woman mumbling largesse until Nicole wanted to thump her into silence. After a keen appraisal of the ground floor, during which she was privately certain Drew had not overlooked a single nut or bolt, he headed for the staircase.

'Er—could I have a word?' Nicole asked, putting a hand on Mrs Foster's arm to cut short her eager path to Drew's side. She waited until he had safely disappeared upstairs, then said, 'Please may I have the rent?'

'Of course, dear.' Her tenant pulled open the drawer of a small bureau and took out a bundle of notes. 'My husband's working at the factory again, I'm pleased to say, so next month we hope to pay off the backlog. After that there shouldn't be any more hiccups. The big American order came in and he's been getting plenty of overtime. He's working this afternoon.' She smiled happily as she handed over the money. 'He's finished the decorating and the wall by the stream.'

A tour of the cottage followed, and Nicole was delighted with the fresh wallpaper. Later the three of them walked to the foot of the garden where trailing orange and yellow nasturtiums and blue lobelia spilled from beds atop the rough stone wall. Nicole smiled her pleasure. Mr Foster had added both protection and a picturesque feature to her garden, surely that would help the sale of the cottage?

'Well built,' was Drew's comment as he prodded it with the toe of his shoe. He frowned at the stream beyond, babbling cheerfully around mossy boulders. 'Has that ever caused trouble?'

Before she could reply Mrs Foster embarked on her version of the flood, larding it freely with exaggerated descriptions of the damage and the problems Nicole had surmounted in setting everything to rights. Drew became thoughtful, but offered no comment, turning instead to stride around the perimeter of the lawn, jabbing out questions which Nicole answered only because it would have been petty to argue in front of a third party. The exterior of the cottage received a similar scrutiny. By the time they took their leave from a beaming Mrs Foster she was seething. It was *her* cottage. True, he was entitled to check that it was capable of raising the money she owed him, but one glance proved that. There was no call for his sharp-eyed assessment. Angrily Nicole stomped ahead to the car.

'Happy now?' she snapped as he turned the ignition. 'You've had a damn good look over *my* house. Are you satisfied I can raise four thousand pounds?' She paused and added sharply, 'Plus the price of the contact lenses?'

He threw her a reproving glance, but remained silent as they drove away from the cottage and Mrs Foster, who was waving gaily, entreating Drew to, 'Call again, any time you like.'

There was a long corner, a narrow humped-back bridge and the lane straightened out, running between green meadows where cattle ruminated in the sunshine. Drew swung the car on to the wide grass verge and switched off the engine. Hooking an arm along the back of her seat, he turned. 'Don't sell the cottage, it has tremendous possibilities.'

The windows had been wound down and a warm breeze sifted through Nicole's hair. Automatically she pushed the silken fringe off her brow. 'I must, I need the money.' There was a stubborn line to her jaw.

'Then sell it to me, I'll give you a fair price.'

A mutinous whisper sounded inside her head. *'No!'*

'For Pete's sake, Nicole, I'm trying to help. I'll give you a fair market price.' A whip-lick of irritation crossed Drew's face, and he caught hold of her shoulders.

Raising her chin, she glared at him. 'No. No, thank you.'

'Okay,' he said coldly. 'Go ahead, self-destruct. Sell your damn cottage if you can, though you'll lose money on the deal. Mortgages are hard to come by on old properties and there can't be too many folk around willing to splurge on accommodation which will require new electric wiring and treatment for dry rot within the next year or so.'

The grey-green eyes skidded to his in alarm. 'But you approve of Honeysuckle Haven. You agree it has possibilities.'

'So it does, but there are some problems which need to be ironed out. If the average buyer reads "dry rot" on a surveyor's report, he runs a mile.'

'Oh!' Her anger collapsed like a pack of cards, to be quickly replaced by creeping panic.

Drew tilted his head to one side. 'Will you consider my offer?'

'I will.' She was fretting at the prospect of the cottage proving unsaleable when another thought popped into her mind. 'Why did you tell Mrs Foster you were my fiancé?'

'It occurred to me that it could be an eminently suitable arrangement. You owe me, so I might as well accrue a little interest.' Drew edged closer, one hand sliding on to her midriff, his fingers brushing the lower swell of her breast. Nicole was suddenly conscious that his mouth was only inches from hers, and as his thigh rubbed hers, she trembled. He smiled at her reaction.

'For years I've been under pressure from my family to settle down. If I produce a fiancée they'll get off my back for a while. Also an announcement in the press will help to nullify the image of me as a playboy.' He lifted a self-mocking brow. 'I detest that particular tag and something as conventional as an engagement will help to set the record straight. In any case, you know darn well how I feel about you, and I have a pretty fair idea of how you feel about me.' He took hold of her hand and guided it towards the buttons on his shirt. 'Touch me,' he murmured.

Fingers spread taut like a starfish, Nicole pushed against the iron-hard muscles, but Drew chuckled and held her close against him, bending to kiss her.

'No!' she protested, wrenching her head from side to side in an attempt to avoid the plundering mouth, but she was trapped, and the kiss became a reality. Rough bristles jarred across her upper lip in a hot moist struggle before her lips parted and she was lost, thrown headlong into a storm-tossed sea of desire from which only Drew could save her. The drugging pressure of his mouth was melting her bones. Now her fingers curled to ease open the buttons and touch the tanned flesh beneath as he had ordered. Drew was hers for the moment, she thought, heart pounding, and it no longer mattered whether he loved her or despised her. A need, strong and unbeatable, united them as the touch of skin-on-skin, mouth-on-mouth, spiralled into exquisite pleasure.

'Darling Nicki,' he murmured, cupping her breast as he teased the hardening pinnacle until she rocked against him.

His kisses were gilding her lips, her eyelids, her jaw, turning her slowly wild with wanting. The hair-sprinkled chest beneath her fingers clenched as she explored the muscled contours.

The noise of an approaching tractor separated them. Drew leaned from her, breathing raggedly, his blue eyes dark with desire, as they waited for the vehicle to pass. At first the waiting was interminable, but it gave Nicole time to come to her senses, and when Drew made as if to pull her back into his arms she backed off.

'It's broad daylight and we're in the car,' she protested, striving for a lightness of tone she did not achieve.

His mouth lurched in rueful agreement and he sighed, watching as she pulled down the sun-visor and began tidying her hair in the mirror.

'You weren't serious about an engagement, were you?' she asked cautiously.

Drew tucked his shirt back into his trousers. 'Why not? I'm not asking you to walk up the aisle, far from it. I merely want you to act as my fiancée until the debt is paid.' He shrugged into the leather jacket. 'I trust you'll co-operate, you must agree I've been very reasonable about your debt so far.'

His tone sounded matter-of-fact, but at the hint of a threat her grey-green eyes clouded. Did she really have much choice? Drew had a ruthless streak, what would happen if she tried to cross him? She inspected her watch. It was too late now to visit the estate agent and set the sale of the cottage in motion, but she would be knocking on his door first thing Monday morning. Perhaps she would strike lucky and sell Honeysuckle Haven to the first person who came to view; for she would do all she could to dispose of it herself, she refused to consider Drew's offer. And as soon as the cottage was sold and the money repaid, she could discover exactly where she stood in his estimation. Maybe he would discard her, once she was free, but that was a risk she would have to take.

Drew dragged back the hair from his temples with both hands. 'Do you play it my way?'

Despite her outward air of calm, her heart was skittering madly. If she refused perhaps he *would* make trouble. Suppose the newspapers got hold of the story and Charlie's name was bandied around—linked with her mother's! The gutter press would have a field day. Nicole took a deep breath. 'I'll agree to an engagement to be announced in the newspapers, but that's all—no ring, no—no complications.' She wasn't sure what complications she envisaged, but knowing Drew anything was possible. She set her lips into a determined line. 'And the engagement is cancelled the minute I repay the money.'

He grinned cheerfully. 'Whatever you say, poppet.'

Nicole had expected he would drive her straight back to the bedsit, but instead he followed the country lanes until they reached the River Thames. Taking her hand, he showed her a deserted towpath and they strolled along in the tranquil golden glow of the late afternoon. She began to relax. Drew was good company, he made her laugh and they found plenty to discuss. Time slipped away. When evening came he drove them to a riverside pub for drinks and dinner, and Nicole admitted to herself that she hadn't had so much fun since ... No, not since Roberto. His fun had been strictly physical, depending on the spice of sex to keep their relationship alive. With Drew it was different, though the sensual tie between them was intrinsic dynamite kept carefully under control. A casual brush of his hair against her brow or the touch of his fingers had them both gazing at each other a little too intently before their eyes bounced apart. But there was something deeper than mere physical attraction, and Nicole wished she could understand.

Now that she had accepted that she loved him she began to wonder why. Drew was attractive to women, that much was patently obvious, but so were many

other men. His low-key sense of humour appealed to
her. She liked his style, the ease with which he
conducted himself, and she liked the way his hair curled
on to the back of his neck, the arrogant line of his jaw,
the crinkle of his eyes when he laughed. Oh no, she
thought, what will I do when he leaves me? With Drew
she felt safe, though safe seemed an odd reaction
considering she was at his mercy, and there was no
doubt he was capable of slashing back if she refused to
obey his wishes. Safe could not apply to a man who
harboured such ambivalent feelings towards her—could
it?

It was dark when Drew parked outside the rooming-
house. Street lights cast stark pools of white on littered
gutters, broken-hinged gates, cracked window panes;
the ravages of time on a down-at-heel neighbourhood.
No wide-eyed children surfaced to watch the arrival of
the Jaguar, instead ominous youths in black leather
scowled from gloomy doorways.

'Thank you for a lovely day,' Nicole smiled, meaning
every word.

She felt mellow and happy, at peace with the world
and, strangely, with Drew.

He frowned at the garbage spilling from dustbins in
the sinister shadows. 'Go and collect your things,' he
ordered, rubbing uneasily at his jaw. 'I'm not leaving
you here in this ghetto tonight. You're coming home
with me.'

CHAPTER SEVEN

'DON'T be silly!' Nicole scoffed. 'I've lived here for months and never come to any harm.'

Drew trickled his fingers across the smooth plane of her cheek. 'Poppet, it's you who's being silly. You march around flashing that damn great diamond in a slum like this and you honestly believe everyone wishes you well? Wise up. One of these days you'll be trotting off to buy crisps, looking like a million dollars as usual, when there'll be one hell of a crack on the back of your head. The diamond will have vanished when you wake up and who knows what state you'll be in.' He tapped an impatient tune on the steering wheel. 'I don't suppose they taught you much about grievous bodily harm at boarding school?'

She tossed back a strand of russet-brown hair. 'Stop exaggerating!'

'I'm not. Would you risk leaving this car parked at the kerb for more than five minutes?' he demanded, and when she was forced to admit she wouldn't, he continued, 'then use your common sense. Think how much easier it is to grab a diamond than a whole motor car.'

'But I shall be safe upstairs in my room!'

He frowned, disturbed by her innocence.

'So some yobbo has followed you to find out where you live. He barges in through the front door and threatens your landlady. Do you imagine she's going to risk getting hurt on your account? Like hell! She'll show him your room, sit tight and swear blind she never heard a thing when the police arrive.'

On cue two youths with shaved heads sauntered

from the shadows to weave a hostile path towards the car, making Nicole instinctively raise her hands to cover the diamond on its slender golden chain. As they passed they hooted with malevolent laughter, and she shuddered. Subconsciously she had been aware of the underlying threat of danger in the neighbourhood, especially after dark, but she had refused to consider it until now.

'I'll check into a hotel for tonight,' she decided as the youths were joined by two more at the street corner.

'Don't waste money. There's a spare bedroom at my apartment, and we *are* engaged as far as outsiders are concerned—right?'

Nicole chewed her lip in indecision.

'No one's going to hold up their hands in horror, this is the permissive age,' he drawled. 'And we're both adults, or at least *I* am. You, I wonder about at times.'

She pouted at his comment. Who was going to criticise if she spent the night under Drew's roof? No one would know, no one would care. Nobody cared about her now that Charlie had gone. A sob ached in her throat, but she gulped it away. All she had to do was make certain that it was the spare room, and not *his* room, she slept in, but that should be no problem. In her heart of hearts she knew Drew would never force himself upon her, he was far too proud for that. The blood pounded in her head—the only danger could be from her *own* desires. Nicole surveyed the dingy rooming house. One thing was certain, she had no wish to spend another night in there.

'Can you manage to bring all your luggage?' he asked when she gave her agreement. 'I'd carry the cases down myself, but I'm uneasy about leaving the car.' He scowled at the gang of youths. 'Tomorrow we'll find you somewhere decent.'

The spurt of adrenaline caused by speculative glances from the street corner, and the wish for Drew and his car to remain in one piece, lasted long enough for Nicole to garble apologies to her landlady and collect her belongings. Her departure was so rapid that only when the car disappeared around the corner did the woman realise Nicole had gone forever and begin to curse.

Drew's apartment was a palace compared to the cramped bedsit. It comprised the first floor of a four-storied Georgian house in an elegant London square. A small park with lawns and statues surrounded by flower-beds graced the centre of the square and sycamore trees swayed in the glow of the street lights.

A uniformed porter, who had insisted on dealing with her luggage, travelled with them in the lift, and Nicole had not known how to react when, in response to the man's cheery greetings, Drew had introduced her as his fiancée. The news sparked off delighted congratulations, giving her an inkling of what could happen if the situation was allowed to get out of hand. Uneasily she accepted the man's good wishes and cast Drew a worried glance, but his expression revealed no equivalent hint of disquiet.

However, when the porter bade farewell she was relieved to be classified as Drew's fiancée rather than his—his latest live-in lover, for she had noticed a hint of masculine amusement as the porter touched his peaked cap.

'Enjoy yourselves—sir, madam,' he had said with a cheeky wink.

'Believe me, we will,' Drew returned.

Nicole's temper flared at the innuendo, and in chagrin she flounced away into the spare bedroom where her suitcases were deposited and firmly, and noisily, closed the door.

Like the lounge she had so briefly seen, the bedroom was luxuriously furnished. Heavy glazed-cotton curtains

in pale green and duck-egg blue were pulled across
the casement windows, and there was a shaggy carpet
of a deeper shade of blue. She hung only a couple of
suits at one end of the fitted rosewood wardrobe,
deciding there was little point in unpacking in total
for a one-night stay, and then wondered what to do
next. Idly she dragged her fingertips across the
gleaming dressing-table. All the furniture was well
made and conventional—like Drew, she thought
wryly, then changed her mind. The man behind the
public image could not be so conventional if he was
willing to give house room to a girl he considered to
be a spoiled darling with a dubious background, to
say the least, but whom he desired.

Her tongue clicked in exasperation. If only he would
conceal his desire, for how could she keep her wits
about her when his blue eyes had revealed so eloquently
all evening that he wanted her? The longer they were
together, the more fiercely the fuse of desire had
burned, scorching her until she wanted to thrash
impatiently, knowing it was safer to be free—free of
Drew, and yet not wanting to be. Nicole tightened her
lips. There was only one thing to do—return to the
lounge, thank him for his hospitality and beat a hasty
retreat.

But it was not as simple as that. When she hesitantly
re-emerged Drew was sprawled, long legs thrust out
before him, at one end of a plushy gold sofa.

Smiling, he flung out a hand in welcome. 'Come on
in, poppet.'

She took reluctant steps across the thick Chinese
carpet. The room was large and oak-panelled, one wall
filled with shelves bursting with books of all sizes and
colours. The sofa, flanked by armchairs in the same
golden hue, faced a marble fireplace and set in the
grate, where logs would flame in winter, was an
extravagant arrangement of crimson and white full-

blown roses. As Nicole walked forward their heady fragrance filled her nostrils.

Drew got to his feet. 'What will you have to drink?'

She halted before him. 'Nothing, thank you. I'm— I'm tired, I'll be off to bed now.' When she tried to produce a yawn she failed miserably, and something like a grin appeared at the corner of Drew's mouth. Regardless, she held out a polite hand. 'You've been very kind and I appreciate it. Thank you. Goodnight.' She was doling out the words in teaspoons.

He chuckled. 'My goodness, why are you so formal all of a sudden? You'll be writing me a thank-you letter next!' He jerked his head towards the sofa. 'Sit down. Kick off your shoes and relax, it's Sunday in the morning, so you can have a lie-in. We both can. Now, what would you like—whisky, gin, brandy?'

Sitting primly, Nicole said, 'I'll have a small sherry please.'

She reminded herself of a maiden aunt, and the idea seemed to strike Drew, for when he handed her the sherry he was wearing a broad grin.

'Chin up, Nicki, I'm not going to eat you—yet!'

Hot and cold all over, she gulped in a rash mouthful which went down the wrong way. Coughing and spluttering, she flushed bright pink. Calmly Drew took the glass and patted her back, while she gasped for air like a hooked fish. His closeness, and the rub of his large hand on her shoulderblades, made it harder to gain her equilibrium.

'I'm fine,' she assured him finally.

'You're not supposed to swig it back like brown ale,' he mocked, smiling as she retrieved her glass.

Nicole had a careful sip. Once the sherry disappeared so would she. 'I want to go to bed,' she explained.

Drew slid an arm around her shoulders and pulled her to him. 'So do I.'

It took all the strength she could muster to ignore the

double meaning, for his long fingers were tapping out a silent rhythm on her shoulder, creating a delicious tingle that rippled all the way down to her toes. She studied the amber liquid. If she met his gaze she would be too starry-eyed to control her own destiny. She took another sip of sherry, and another, and another, scarcely noticing the fiery path the liquid traced along her throat. The glass was empty.

'That was—good,' she said lamely, setting it aside. She made as if to move, but the fingers on her shoulder tightened. Discarding his own tumbler, Drew rubbed his forehead against hers in slow desire.

'Aren't you going to give me a goodnight kiss?' he murmured.

There was a trace of musk oil on his skin, whisky warm on his breath. A terrifying contraction cramped Nicole's heart as he lazily reached out to run his index finger along the line of her jaw.

'Drew, you're not playing fair,' she protested as desire quivered through her.

'I'm not playing.'

He reached out, gathering her into his arms and silencing her protests with deep kisses. He framed her face with his hands, while his eager mouth roamed over her skin, inflaming her until she trembled. He moved his hands lower, rubbing the pads of his thumbs on the sensitive cords of her throat.

'Nicki darling, I—I——' he whispered.

She had difficulty in breathing. Say it, Drew, she implored silently, say that you love me.

He bent to kiss the scooped-out hollow of her collarbone. 'I want you so much,' he murmured, though she had the impression it was not what he wanted to say. His mouth slid upwards to cover hers with bruising possession.

Wanting was enough.

Afterwards Nicole could not clearly recall how they

made the journey from the velvety sofa to the silken sheets of his bed. Such details were misty, for Drew had been intent on introducing her to a pagan country where the one inexorable law was pleasure. He kissed her and caressed her, sliding open the zip of her flying suit to explore the heated curves that strained beneath his touch. And when he moaned against her breast that he could wait no longer, she had surrendered to his wishes.

The muted light of a bedside lamp cast bronze shadows on the hard muscles of his shoulders as Nicole stretched up her arms to welcome him.

'Nicki, Nicki,' he muttered raggedly, running his hand along the smooth sweep from her breast to her thigh. 'I want you, my darling. I want you to be a part of me.'

'I am,' she murmured, nibbling at his lips and the prickles of his dark moustache until he gave a moan of complaint and kissed her violently, aggressively, subduing her with a mastery as complete as it was erotic. His long fingers slithered down to possess the golden thrust of her breasts, stroking the pinnacles into rock-hard sensitivity while she cried out at the exquisite torture. His hands moved on firmly to explore the satin clefts and swells, arousing her until their bodies fused, a mutual perspiration blending. Now there was only sensation—Drew's flesh against her flesh, his breath in her mouth, his hard limbs entwined, thrusting to the rhythm of love. A volcano welled up inside her, its molten rivulets drenching her in a fiery embrace. She gasped, her heart beating against his.

'It must be now, my darling,' Drew groaned, as her fingers raked his back. 'Next time —next time it'll be slower, I promise.'

He kept his promise, though afterwards Nicole could not distinguish between the rapid explosion of their first lovemaking and the languid slow-building desire that

followed, for both occasions climaxed in the same
glorious plunge into oblivion.

Sounds of the morning spewed in through the open
window, washing in and out of her subconsciousness
until she came awake. Distant church bells pealed a
welcome to Sunday worshippers, a car droned by,
children were laughing in the square. Nicole yawned,
stretching like a cat, limbs taut, then slack, before
curling up beneath the bedclothes. Beyond the
bathroom door came the sound of Drew humming as
he shaved. My love, she thought, her smile as golden as
the shafts of sunlight flooding the room.

Nicole's smile faltered. Drew was not her love. She
loved him, more completely than ever now she had
given herself to him, but there was no reason to believe
the emotion could be reciprocated. Despondently she
twisted a strand of hair around her finger. Drew had
said he desired her and had proved it beyond all doubt,
but not once in the intimacy of the night had he spoken
of love. Neither had she. She had stifled the words she
longed to whisper, waiting for him to lead the way. She
winced. Some unseen assailant was beating at her brains
with a cudgel and with each blow was the condemnation—stupid, stupid, *stupid*! Drew's vocabulary did not
include love. She had been bewitched by his blue eyes,
confusing the message—for lust she had read love. How
could she have been so shortsighted? He had said he
had no intention of marrying her and agreed that their
relationship should end the minute she was out of his
debt. There were no lines to read between. Drew had
told her he wanted an affair with her—a shortlived one
at that! She meant no more to him that his pop singer,
Tamsin Jay.

Nicole's immediate reaction was to rush into the
bathroom to lambaste him with his sins, but she paused,
tugging uneasily at the strand of hair. Would not Drew

respond, with good reason, that his sins were no sins at all? Anyway, she was in no position to risk offending him, for if she did he might deal with her as ruthlessly as he had dealt with Tamsin Jay. What she must do now was build some kind of emotional barrier to protect herself, but before she had time to decide how she could manage to do that the bathroom door swung open and Drew emerged, clad only in blue jeans. He was freshly shaved, his hair combed back from his brow, his tanned skin gleaming. His whole demeanour throbbed with vitality and good health, and she decided that his three weeks of enforced rest had worked wonders.

'How's my gorgeous girl?' he asked, dropping down on the bed and kissing her nose.

'I'm fine. What time is it?' Her tone was light as she adopted a composure she was far from feeling.

'Nearly noon.'

Galvanised into action, Nicole sat upright, holding the sheet protectively over her naked breasts. 'Noon! I must be on my way.'

Why was it she felt like a one-night stand? Her mouth thinned. Perhaps she should ask Drew to knock something off her debt in lieu of services rendered?

'No rush.'

His blue eyes were sending that message again, but now her head was clear and she could decipher properly: l—u—s—t.

Nicole wondered how she could reach the bathroom before he made a grab for her. He was edging dangerously closer, and if he kissed her she knew her wish to avoid further involvement would vanish without trace. Play it cool, her pounding head told her pounding heart as Drew clasped a hand around the back of her neck and gently pulled her to meet his waiting lips. Oh, if he kept on looking at her like that she would die!

'Drew, it's late, I must go and find fresh digs. And then—then I have things to do,' she babbled.

He shook his dark head. 'The only thing you have to do is come out to lunch with me. I rang my mother earlier, she's longing to meet you.'

'No, no!' she cried, horror-struck. 'I'm not hungry.'

'I am.' Firm fingers caught at the top of the sheet and peeled it from her. He smiled, his eyes soft and warm. 'I'm very hungry, poppet, but not for food. So first we'll make me satisfied and then——'

His words petered out as he pushed her down beneath him on to the softness of the bed.

Drew stopped the car beneath a plane tree and came round to open her door. 'Here we are,' he grinned.

Nicole stood on the pavement, surreptitiously eyeing the house before her. Identical with the others along the quiet road, it was a small semi-detached, neatly painted with fresh white net curtains draped at the windows and a regulation square of trimmed lawn surrounded by floribunda roses.

'I really don't think——' she began.

'Stop it!' Drew brushed aside her protestations and took her arm, steering her towards the front gate. 'My mother's waited years for this to happen, so don't spoil it now.'

'But she believes we're really engaged.'

He laughed. 'Of course, that's the whole point.'

'It was to be just an announcement in the newspaper,' she fretted. 'You never said I'd have to meet your family. I feel a fraud. What do I do if they ask when we're—when we're going to be married?'

He wafted a large hand. 'Be vague.'

When a curtain twitched in a window across the street, Drew followed her glance.

'The Jag always causes a bit of a stir, this is strictly cut-price family saloon country. I tried to persuade my mother to move into a bigger and better house, but no go. She couldn't bear to leave her neighbours.' The curtain twitched again and he grinned. 'I could be wrong today. It's probably you who's making the hearts race faster. Sophisticated young women in suede trousers and silk shirts are a rarity—navy nylon anoraks are more the scene.'

Anxiously Nicole glanced down at her bronze shirt and trousers. 'Do you think I'm overdressed?'

'Yes!' He laughed at her look of consternation. 'I much prefer you wearing that diamond of yours—and nothing else.'

'Drew!' she warned, as he slipped an arm around her waist and hugged her to him, but he blithely took no notice, rubbing his moustache against her brow and kissing her before he jammed a finger on the door-bell.

'Don't worry, poppet, they'll love you.'

I don't care whether or not your family love me, she thought miserably, it's *your* love I want.

The front door swung open and they were swept into the hall, where Drew's mother lavished hugs and squeals of welcome with a breathtaking effusiveness. She was small and plump, with wavy grey hair and a happy face glowing her pleasure. Other adults and a gaggle of children hovered in the background, watching the commotion.

'Let's have a look at you,' said Mrs Benedict, standing back and smiling at Nicole. 'Yes, I always said Drew would take his time but pick a winner in the end.'

'And you were right, as usual,' Drew rejoined in mock solemnity.

She patted his hand. 'Perhaps now you'll follow doctor's orders and stop rushing around the world non-stop.' Her eyes narrowed. 'You look peaky, have you been getting enough sleep?'

His blue gaze swung to Nicole. 'Last night was rather—disturbed,' he admitted, the furrow at the side of his mouth deepening.

'Were you celebrating?' his mother asked, immune to the electric current zizzing in the air.

Drew just grinned.

'Yes, we—we went out to dinner,' Nicole put in hurriedly. Drew was going to be no help, standing there all macho male and discreetly triumphant. 'We went to an old country pub by the river.'

Mrs Benedict's ears pricked up and she started to chatter about local restaurants before stopping, mid-flow, when she saw that their audience was still waiting. Then Nicole was introduced, though it was impossible to take in all the names or work out who everyone was. There appeared to be Hugo, his wife and children, Paul and a girl-friend, an uncle, two young cousins and a lady from down the road whose husband was 'off in the Army, so she's needing to be cheered up'. Fortunately Brian was absent, caught up in Portugal on business, and it was a relief not to have to deceive him, too.

A long table, covered with a spotless white damask cloth and many place settings, took up all the available space in the dining-room, and everyone crowded in, sitting where they could. Nicole found herself squashed between Drew and Mandy, Hugo's ten-year-old daughter. Hugo carried in a massive roast and proceeded to carve, passing the plates to his mother, who piled them high with carrots, runner beans, roast potatoes and fluffy Yorkshire pudding.

When everyone was served the eating—and the talking—began. Nicole gazed around in amusement. Now this was a *real* family!

'Ooh, I forgot!' Mrs Benedict squealed, and there was a sudden hush. 'Hugo, go and open up those bottles of wine in the pantry. We must toast the happy couple. Drew, in you go and help him.'

The two men disappeared obediently.

Nicole grew pink with embarrassment, because everyone seemed to be smiling at her.

'When are you and Uncle Drew getting married?' Mandy asked into the silence.

'We haven't decided yet,' she replied, her heart thumping.

'How many bridesmaids will there be, and do they wear long dresses and flowers in their hair?'

There was a hoot of laughter from the end of the table. 'What she really means, my dear, is—is there any chance of her being included?' Mrs Benedict smiled at her granddaughter. 'You've been longing to be a bridesmaid for ages, haven't you, my love?'

'Yes,' whispered Mandy, now flushing as pink as Nicole.

'It's too early to plan bridesmaids yet,' Nicole told the little girl, feeling a flood of shame as Mandy's face filled with disappointment.

'Do you have any sisters or nieces who would like to be bridesmaids?' Drew's mother asked, as everyone resumed their meal.

'No. I'm an only child. My parents are dead, and my one and only aunt lives in Paris!'

Mrs Benedict gasped. 'Paris!'

'The world doesn't stop and start at the white cliffs of Dover,' drawled Drew, coming in with a bottle of wine in each hand.

'Listen to Mr Jet-Setter!' his mother chided, then rested her knife and fork and turned to Nicole. 'So who do you live with, my dear?'

'Nobody.' For some inexplicable reason the admission brought a lump of misery to her throat, and she took a mouthful of the wine Drew had poured to wash it away.

'Nobody?' Mrs Benedict was gasping again. 'But that's dreadful! A young girl like you——' She swung to Drew. 'You can't allow Nicole to live alone. She must move in here with me until the two of you are married.' She grinned back at Nicole. 'I'd be happy to help with the wedding preparations, seeing that you have no mother of your own. You'll look adorable in white.' A thought caught the older woman broadside. 'You've not been married before, have you?'

Drew slammed the empty wine bottle down on the table and everyone froze. 'Discretion is the better part of valour,' he growled. 'You go too far at times, Mum. What damn difference does it make?'

Nicole flashed him a reproving smile and reached for his hand, pulling him down into his chair beside her. 'You'd better not have any more disturbed nights,' she murmured. 'They make you very grumpy.'

Hugo winked at her. 'Too damn true! Behave yourself, little brother.'

'Yes, be good, Uncle Drew,' Mandy piped up, and the other children joined in a chorus of admonition.

Drew ran a hand across his jaw. 'Outnumbered and overruled!' he complained, the corner of his mouth curling into a slow grin of self-derision as his anger dissolved.

'No, I haven't been married before,' Nicole said, smiling at his mother. Mrs Benedict was her friend, they were both on the same side.

'But she's not going to move in here,' Drew continued, determined not to be browbeaten. 'As a matter of fact she's coming to live at my apartment.'

Mrs Benedict cast a wary eye over the children. 'Drew! I don't really think——' she chided.

'Relax,' he said, and squeezed Nicole's hand under the table. She was well aware he was telling her to relax too, for his announcement had tightened her reflexes and she was sitting a little too rigidly in her chair, wondering what was coming next.

'It's all respectable,' he said. 'I'm off to Greece first thing in the morning. But don't forget there are *two* bedrooms and we are going to be married.'

'Where's your ring?' Mandy blurted out, and Nicole was thankful for a change of topic.

'We haven't had time to choose one.'

'That's why Uncle Drew is off to Greece,' Hugo explained, grinning at his daughter. 'He has to earn some more money to buy one.'

Drew raised a brow. 'Damn right—Nicki's an expensive lady to keep.'

She was not quite sure how to take that!

When all the plates had been emptied, Mrs Benedict appeared with a huge apple tart and a pitcher of fresh cream. Cheese and biscuits followed, then coffee. It was mid-afternoon when the men ambled out into the tiny back garden to smoke and argue over the local football team's chances in the League.

Nicole installed herself at the kitchen sink. Smartly dressed she might be, but idle she was not.

'Like cleaning up after a pop festival, isn't it?' Drew's mother commiserated with a glance at the stacked draining-board. 'Wait until you have your own family—but then it's a labour of love.' She put a hand on Nicole's arm. 'You don't know how happy you've made me, my dear. Drew had dragged around for years, scared to death of settling down. It was a tremendous blow to his self-esteem when his first marriage broke up. He considered himself a failure, but it was no more than two youngsters being too immature to cope with married life.' She smiled. 'You must be very special to him.'

Uneasily Nicole concentrated on the washing-up. Drew had been wrong to subject her, and his mother and the rest of his family, to this deception. Already she was regretting the role she was forced to play. A voice came from behind her.

'She is special.' Drew slid his arms around her waist and pulled her back against him, kissing her hair. 'She's been selling my Florida villas for me, she's a clever girl. Three are sold already.'

'Three?' Hands in the washing-up bowl, Nicole twisted to look at him over her shoulder.

'The Whitmans, the French-Canadians and the folk you saw last week. They rang late Friday to commit themselves,' he revealed, grinning at her smile of delight. 'Mr and Mrs Purdy are still wavering.'

'Huh, holiday villas for people with money to burn,' his mother grumbled, but they could tell she was secretly proud. 'Who needs all that sunshine? What's wrong with Eastbourne?'

'Nicole needs the sunshine—you should see her spectacular suntan,' Drew murmured, nibbling at her earlobe and lighting another fuse of delicious desire which she rapidly doused.

The afternoon drifted on to four o'clock when Mrs Benedict produced hot scones with lashings of strawberry jam and cream, and although everyone patted their stomachs and professed to be full from lunch, the scones disappeared in quick-fire succession. Afterwards somebody decreed that exercise was vital, and they all poured out of the house and around the corner to start a noisy game of French cricket in the local park. Mandy had taken a liking to Nicole, and hung on to her hand, whisperings schoolgirl secrets, much to Drew's amusement. The mood was free and easy. Hugo and Paul and their ladies were friendly, everyone chatted with everyone else, and for the first time in her life Nicole felt she was part of a family group, a feeling which made joy sing in her heart. Now she knew what her past had lacked, what Charlie had yearned to create for her—but had only halfway succeeded.

The ease with which Drew fitted into the scene surprised her. She had known him as the businessman, the harsh interrogator, the lover, and now there was a further side to his personality, that of family man. His relationship with his brothers was close. They insulted and praised each other with equal diffidence, and the fact that Hugo was on a far lower scale financially was irrelevant; he argued his views with equal gusto.

'My turn, my turn!' one of Hugo's boys cried, then squealed with laughter as Drew upended him.

'Whose turn?' he demanded in mock rage.

'Yours, Uncle Drew,' came the giggled reply as the child was lifted high into the air.

'I expect you'll want to start a family straight away?' Hugo's wife whispered. 'Drew's great with kids, our three adore him.'

The conversation was moving too fast.

'Er—we've not talked about that,' Nicole confessed, wishing she could abandon the deception. She was enjoying herself, but the longer she and Drew were together with his family, the worse their deceit became and now she knew it was wrong.

'We must go,' said Drew when they returned from the park.

His mother's face fell. 'Stay a little longer, we're just getting to know Nicki.'

'Can't. We have things to arrange,' he said flatly.

'Persuade him, Nicki,' Mrs Benedict pleaded. 'Or at least make him say when you'll be coming again. Drew's a devil for refusing to be pinned down. Why don't you come round one evening next week while he's away, and——'

'We can't fix anything right now,' Drew cut in.

Nicole stood on the sidelines feeling mean. No way would she repeat the visit, it had been too pleasant and yet too harrowing. She had been given a glimpse of what her life could have included if circumstances had been different, and the knowledge was tearing her heart to shreds. In the end it was she who turned away towards the car, with Drew following a moment later.

'Families!' he complained, as the Jaguar leapt away from the waving throng. He ran a hand through his rumpled hair. 'Everyone is so damned interested, they want to run your life for you!'

'It's better than not having anyone who cares,' Nicole retorted, sitting stiffly beside him. A scornful grunt was his only response. 'Today was a mistake,' she brooded. 'I felt so—so shoddy, receiving all those genuine good wishes.' She glared at him. 'Poor Mandy is hoping to be a bridesmaid, and soon! And—and the next time you visit your mother she'll want to know all the details and you'll have made things ten times worse for yourself, not better, and——' The final phrase jerked out. 'And it serves you right!'

Drew kept silent, so Nicole ignored him, staring out of the car, seeing nothing.

Finally he spoke. 'If things get too hot I'll just have to produce you again, won't I?'

'Oh no! Once I've paid off the money I'm going. Wild horses wouldn't drag me back to take part in such a pointless shabby charade.'

Drew's hands tightened on the wheel. 'Maybe Charles Werner has left a trail of unpaid bills in other countries, too. If I'm good enough to settle those, then you'll still be in my debt, won't you?'

Images raced through her head like an overwound film. She could not bear it if he was correct and mud was thrown all over Charlie's memory.

'I don't believe he left any more debts,' she said staunchly. 'He was always very concerned about right and wrong.' She scowled at the sceptical lift to Drew's brow. 'The Tenerife bills must have been an oversight.'

'Four thousand pounds is one hell of an oversight!'

Nicole's chin jutted. 'He was a dying man, and ill-health changes people. Perhaps he imagined he had settled the bills when he hadn't.'

Knowing Charlie's mania for doing everything properly, it didn't sound convincing, even to her, and she was not surprised when Drew let out a sarcastic breath.

'This is all supposition, let's leave it for now,' he said.

'Okay,' she conceded, too weary to argue further, and as they drove along she rested her head against the side window, the cool glass balm to her burning brow. 'Why did your mother wonder if I'd been married before?' she asked, after a while.

Drew's jaw tensed. 'Because a few years ago she discovered I was dating a divorcee, and she didn't like it. My mother's from the old school, she believes all marriages are made in heaven. She frowns on divorce.' He gave a bark of grim laughter. 'Though she was forced to reconsider her views when Karen and I split up. She was very fond of Karen—still is. Mind you, she hates to confess that one of her sons had a marriage that went rapidly downhill.' There was a steel thread in his voice.

'But young marriages are risky, statistics prove that. The younger you are, the more chance there is of divorce. How old were you when you married?'

'Twenty.'

Nicole tilted her head and surveyed him. 'And what were you like at twenty?'

'An arrogant fool.'

'Like you are now?'

Drew grinned, and the tension evaporated. For the remainder of the journey they had a comfortable discussion of their visit, until Nicole discovered she was showering his family with too much praise and decided she must cool down.

Drew fished the keys out of his pocket and unlocked the door to his apartment.

'May I take a look at the Yellow Pages and use the phone?' Nicole enquired, walking in before him.

He shrugged. 'Yes, but why?'

'To fix fresh accommodation.'

'You don't need it, poppet,' he said, strolling up to

kiss her forehead. 'You're staying here while I'm away, as I told my mother.'

'No, I can't.' She twisted from his embrace.

'Why not? The apartment will be empty, so what's the point in wasting good money on a hotel? Your frivolous days are over, Nicki—at least, for the time being.'

Resenting the warning tone of voice, she glared at him, but Drew was unconcerned.

'Besides, I'd like to know you're safe. The porter will keep an eye on you.'

Uneasily she chewed at the inside of her lip. 'I don't think we ought to get any more—involved.'

'In what way?' he asked, but the burn of his blue eyes indicated he knew exactly what she meant.

'If I stay here tonight, you'll want to—to make love?'

'Yes.'

'I'd rather we didn't,' she lied, feeling her face flush. 'I'm tired.'

'Isn't a headache the usual excuse?' Drew's tone was flippant, but she sensed the muted hostility. He turned towards his room. 'Don't worry, I shan't bother you. I'll collect some papers and go to the office, there are several reports I must deal with before I depart in the morning.' He strode away, stopping with his hand on the door knob. 'There's food in the kitchen if you want to fix something to eat. Don't bother to wait up, it'll be late when I get home.'

Nicole went to bed at ten, but sleep proved elusive. She heard a distant church clock chime one, and still Drew had not returned. When she awoke in the morning the apartment was quiet, and she crept around on tiptoe until she discovered a note which indicated he had been and gone. The keys were there and various instructions on how the apartment, the maid service, the porterage facility and the car parking operated. Keys to the

Jaguar had been left, too, but she decided she would not take advantage of his generosity in that department at least.

A quick forage of the kitchen revealed all the necessary ingredients for breakfast, and when she had eaten she made a shopping list. She would not use Drew's food, either. He was due home the following Monday, and she decided to leave on Sunday. If she was in residence when he returned there was no doubt he would inveigle her to stay, and then she would find herself back in his bed.

'No,' she said out loud. 'An on-off affair is not my scene.'

Mid-morning she took the bus and travelled out to see the estate agent through whom she had purchased Honeysuckle Haven. The man, previously an optimist, was now a pessimist, and it was remarkable how the cottage's advantages had switched to *dis*advantages. When he had sold her the property he had counted its antiquity as a plus, now it was a minus. Likewise the remote position, once praised, became a liability, and although he did not mention rewiring and dry rot, she had no doubt he was saving them for a later attack.

'We'll do our best,' he promised mournfully, as he showed her the door. 'But don't expect a quick sale.'

Now it was difficult to keep her spirits buoyant, and when she bought a newspaper to study the 'situations vacant', depression loomed. But it is Monday, she told herself as she pored over the columns. Everyone knew choice jobs came nearer the weekend, or did they? She could not afford to be out of work for too long, her money would disappear like magic if she was not earning. She wrinkled her nose at the mediocre jobs with their mediocre salaries. The Benedict post had been one in a million, it was impossible to strike so lucky twice in a row. Dispiritedly she circled a couple of vacancies which were vaguely interesting.

Drew had not mentioned her resignation, but she presumed another girl had been trained and was perhaps, even now, winging her way across the Atlantic. She wondered how José, Rochelle and Jean would react to her replacement, for she had taken the coward's way out and not mentioned her resignation to anyone. An empty feeling gnawed at her stomach as she considered the newcomer. Key Benedict was *her* island, and the villas *her* villas!

When she opened the curtains on Tuesday morning it was raining. The sky was hung with dark grey clouds, water was dripping off the trees in the square and Nicole's precarious spirits plunged further. She had talked herself into telephoning the two job vacancies, when a ring came at the door-bell.

'Hello!' she said, wide-eyed and smiling, for Brian stood there.

'Congratulations, I hear you're about to become my sister-in-law—that's wonderful! Drew's shown some sense at long last.' He leaned forward to kiss her cheek, and then followed her into the lounge, dropping down on to the sofa, his boyish face alive with pleasure.

Nicole was torn between delight at seeing him again and the uncomfortable role she was forced to play, for Brian started to regale her with stories of his family's happiness over the news of the engagement.

'My mother's in the seventh heaven,' he chuckled. 'When I rang her last night she was bubbling over. She reckons you're perfect for Drew.' Nicole inspected her fingernails. 'I must confess the news took me by surprise,' he continued.

'It did me, too,' Nicole burst out, not thinking.

Brian's hazel eyes were merry. 'The Florida sunshine obviously did the trick. Now Drew'll be able to stop roaming around like a lost soul, thank heavens. Incidentally, I wouldn't be surprised if my mother decided to pop round here unannounced—she's longing to hear more details.'

'Would you like a cup of coffee?' Nicole asked, desperate to break the thread of conversation.

'No, thanks.' He became serious. 'Actually I've not come only to offer my congratulations, I want to beg a favour.'

'And what's that?' She prayed it would not involve her in more deception.

Brian shifted forward, clasping his hands between his knees. 'We've hit a snag. I realise you're having a few days off, buying your trousseau and so on——'

Her eyes widened. 'I am?'

'Drew spoke to me yesterday,' he continued earnestly. 'He explained how you were staying here in order to do some shopping and start preparations for your wedding, and he told me not to trouble you with business matters. I know you'll be back at the office next week, but this morning I had an urgent phone call from some friends of Sir William Whitman, a Mr and Mrs Drysdale. It appears they know about the Key Benedict villas and are anxious to see them. The problem is that the husband is a very busy man, and is only free right now.' He rose to his feet and paced before her. 'Drew will be furious I'm asking you this, but I wondered if you would be prepared to fly over to Florida with them tomorrow. They're already favourably disposed towards the villas, and you could be there and back in a few days. It seems a pity at best to delay a sale, or at worst to miss one.'

As he smiled down at her, Nicole's mind whirled. So Drew had not told Brian about her resignation, and no other girl had been employed in her place. Drew was stringing her along, but why?

'We needn't tell Drew you're going,' Brian coaxed. 'If he wonders where you are I'll say you've been busy celebrating. And he'll be delighted when you pull off another sale.'

Nicole coiled a stray tendril of glossy brown hair around her finger, her eyes lowered in thought. If she remained at the apartment Drew's mother might arrive and then she would be forced into more lies. The prospect of further falsehood made her squirm. And what would happen if Drew himself came back unexpectedly? She had no illusions about her strength of resistance. He would look at her with those expressive blue eyes and she would be lost. Nicole came to a decision. She would go to Florida, if only to avoid his mother. And when she came home she would make certain no one knew her flight time on landing, and would disappear into the crowds and make a fresh start away from Drew.

'Fine, I'd be happy to help,' she said. 'I'd rather we kept it a secret from Drew until afterwards—I'd like to surprise him.' She gave a shaky laugh. 'The sale would be like a sort of—wedding present.'

'Good idea,' Brian agreed. 'You'll be there and back before he knows it. He's telephoning this afternoon from Tenerife, but I won't say a word.'

'Tenerife? But I understood he was in Greece?' Nicole said faintly.

There was a firm shake of the head. 'No, Tenerife, though I've no idea why. We have an excellent man in charge of operations out there and rarely have any problems. The last crisis was over a year ago.'

Her stomach plunged; she knew exactly what was coming next.

'There was a fellow called Werner who had been a good customer of ours for years and we thought he was reliable, but—wham!' Brian hit his fist into his palm and made her jump nervously. 'Without warning he disappeared and left one hell of a bill.'

'And Drew was furious,' she gulped, grateful that Brian knew nothing about her role in the affair.

He made a vague gesture of indifference. 'Like all

large companies we have an annual margin allotted to bad debts, so it was written off before tax. Drew's always philosophical about these things—bad debts are a fact of life.'

Nicole stared at him. 'But didn't he take steps to try and trace Mr Werner?'

'Drew's far too busy to waste time chasing up bad debts,' Brian said offhandedly. 'And as he pointed out, the fellow had been one of our best customers for years, so in the long run we didn't come out of it too badly.'

For a dazed moment she stared at him, then a question mark appeared in her brain. Why had Drew insisted that the debt had been so devastating, when now it seemed to have been accepted as little more than an irritation?

CHAPTER EIGHT

SWAYING lances of palm-trees waved Nicole a welcome as the Cadillac sped along the causeway. On either side was a deep blue expanse of water, polka-dotted with sails of yachts and windsurfers, while jet-skis zig-zagged among the craft, foamy white plumes rearing behind like exotic tail feathers. Beside her José whistled contentedly, half obliterating the 'oohs' and 'ahs' from Mrs Drysdale as she surveyed the scene. Nicole gave a soft sigh of pleasure. It was good to be back, whatever the circumstances.

'Somebody's para-sailing!' the older woman exclaimed, and heads craned to monitor the progress of a red, white and blue parachute across the sky.

José raised a hand to return the security guard's greeting as they approached the gatehouse, and seconds later they passed between twin granite pillars carved with gold lettering. Nicole turned to smile.

'Welcome to Key Benedict.'

Identical grins of happy anticipation greeted her words as the Drysdales noted the emerald swoop of the golf course on the left, the showy displays of scarlet hibiscus and tropical vines in gardens to the right.

Mr Drysdale, a cheerful balding man in his late fifties, settled back in his seat. 'We're going to like it,' he prophesied comfortably, and Nicole gave a silent agreement.

The Drysdales were as pleasant as the Whitmans had been and she knew they would fall in love with the villas. Four sales in less than two months! Whatever Drew's opinion of her as a person, he could not fail to agree that she had excelled in selling the villas. Though

172

what Drew thought of her, deep down, remained a
mystery.

As it had done since her conversation with Brian,
Nicole's mind continued to tack violently between
optimism and gloom. Was Drew using Charlie's debt to
manacle her to him for some private reason of his own?
Memories of their lovemaking floated to the surface.
How avid and tender he had been; surely he must feel
something for her? But perhaps she was deceiving
herself. It was possible his contempt for the 'spoiled rich
girl' image had sparked off a ruthless desire to make her
pay. Drew had had to fight to reach the top. He was a
self-made man, with a status in life directly attributable
to his own efforts, and no one else's. She did not blame
him for casting a scornful eye on those who wallowed in
inherited luxury without lifting a finger, and in her case
the luxury had not even been inherited. It had been
provided by an old man whose motives had been
blameless, but did Drew believe that? The only reason
he had gone to Tenerife must be to delve further into
Charlie's past—and her own.

The depths of the grey-green eyes flashed with yellow
daggers. To hell with Drew and his doubting mind! She
had done nothing to be ashamed of, and she was
convinced that Charlie, too, would prove to have an
unsullied history. The Tenerife debts had been the
aberration of a dying man, that was all.

Over the following days, the pace was hot. Delighted
approval greeted the villas, as expected, and because the
Drysdales were eager to set the deal in motion, meetings
had to be organised to arrange financial matters. Mrs
Drysdale expressed her own ideas on furnishing,
prompting Nicole to spend long hours shepherding her
client between interior decorators and department
stores. Pushing her trepidation to one side, she had
refused José's offer to repeat his performance as

chauffeur and, after a few false starts, had managed to acquire the knack of American driving.

Mr Drysdale turned out to be a keen sailor, so one morning they had left at the crack of dawn to visit a boat builder in Indian River County. With a temperature nudging the nineties and high humidity, it was a hot sticky day and Nicole gratefully followed local fashion, wearing only a brief white ribbed suntop and matching shorts. In response to Mr Drysdale's interest in one of the gleaming-hulled launches, a demonstration sail was offered, and after listening to the salesman's spiel for a few minutes Nicole lost interest, sloping off to stretch out on the salt-splashed decks and drowse.

Hours in the sun and the whip of the surf had gilded her skin to a dusky gold when she dropped her clients back at the hotel in the early evening. She was tired, but happy. Well, almost . . . thoughts of Drew continued to plague her, but as she parked the huge Cadillac, she successfully stifled them.

Workmen on high ladders were fixing a gold and white tasselled banner across the hotel entrance, and Nicole paused, waiting for it to be unfurled.

'Meet Tamsin Jay in Cabaret', it suggested.

She rocked back in surprise. Tamsin Jay! If Drew had once ejected the singer from his life now, perhaps, she was being reinstated! Nicole frowned as she walked into the hotel lobby, but then the lines smoothed from her brow. She was presuming too much. The Benedict company controlled a profusion of hotels, but no way would Drew, as Chairman, bother himself with their cabaret programmes; entertainment managers would control that department. And yet . . .

Key Benedict was special to him. Might he not keep an eye on all the activities on the island, including the choice of cabaret artists? It struck her that he could be planning to resurrect his affair with the singer once she herself had

faded from the scene. What better way of climbing back
into favour than offering Tamsin a top slot?

'We have a soulmate of yours here,' the desk clerk
grinned, as Nicole collected her room key. He nodded
towards a glamour pin-up of Tamsin Jay. 'Another
English miss. If all the girls on the far side of the
Atlantic are as pretty as you two, I guess it's time I
hightailed it over there!'

Nicole offered a tepid smile. She had no wish to be
coupled with the singer, though it was fair to say they
had something in common; they had both met Drew
and both lived to regret it . . .

'Must confess Tamsin Jay's a new name to me,' the
man continued chattily. 'But I hear she's hot stuff in
your country.'

'I believe so.'

Nicole cast a wry glance at the photograph which
depicted a golden-haired temptress with high cheekbones, huge eyes and flawless complexion. Anyone can
be made to look beautiful in a photograph, she decided
waspishly, refusing to accept that Tamsin Jay could be
quite as stunning in real life.

'If you want to take a look, she's rehearsing in the
restaurant,' the desk clerk grinned.

Uncertainly Nicole sauntered away across the
polished pine floor. What did Tamsin Jay really look
like? What kind of woman could gain Drew's attention
and then be offloaded with no further ado because she
breached a need for public respectability? She swithered.
Should she take a look, or did it make more sense to
banish thoughts of Drew, and all things connected with
Drew, from her mind?

Feminine curiosity propelled her towards the heavy
oak doors of the main restaurant. When she slipped in
between them, it was into gloom, and she stood
blinking. The carpeted tiers of tables and chairs were
dark, but in the centre of the vast room a battery of

spotlights lit an elevated stage where a shapely blonde
stood before a small group of musicians.

'One, two, three,' came the instruction, and the band
started into a throbbing blues number.

As Nicole's eyes adjusted, she sagged inside. Tamsin
Jay *was* as beautiful as her photograph. She was
prowling around the stage like a jungle creature in a
body-hugging leopard-skin leotard and black tights,
displaying the longest legs Nicole had ever seen.
Appropriately the song was about luring men into her
den, and as she strutted, prancing and spitting, Tamsin
tossed the honey-coloured hair around her shoulders
like a glossy hurricane. Mesmerised, Nicole crept
forward through the deserted ranks of tables to sink
down on to a velvet banquette.

'Fantastic!' the lead guitarist exclaimed, giving a final
twang as the song ended.

Tamsin Jay stood, hands on hips, panting and
smiling out into the darkness. 'Did you like me?' she
enquired.

Nicole now noticed a shadowy figure sitting beyond
the glare of the lights, and when a sombre-suited giant
pushed himself out of his chair, her eyes narrowed in
alarm. The height and proud angle of the gipsy-dark
head were unmistakable, making her heart bounce
uncontrollably within her breast as though a basketball
player was slapping it with the flat of his hand.

'Great performance, you'll wow them,' said Drew,
smiling up at the breathless blonde.

'Darling, help me down,' she murmured, holding out
her arms.

Obediently he reached to swing her easily from the
stage and Nicole froze as their two bodies met—
feminine leopard-skin curves slithering against the hard
male physique. Somehow Tamsin lingered in his arms a
moment too long before turning back to the band.

'That's all for now, boys. We'll have a final run

through tomorrow.' She linked an arm through Drew's and said clearly, 'It was sweet of you to fly over here especially to see me, darling.'

With an enigmatic smile Drew extricated himself from the blonde's embrace.

'Come down here, Nicki. I'd like to introduce you,' he called into the darkness.

Nicole's body clenched like a fist. How did he know she was there? She had crept silently into the darkened restaurant, believing herself to be an audience of one, but all the while Drew had been there, *and* he had noticed her arrival. Tousled and sunburnt, in flat sandals, she was no physical match for the glamorous Tamsin, and she began to wish fervently that a genie would appear to magic her away. She knew she looked like some windswept waif from the shore, and had no wish to meet Tamsin. What was more, she had no wish to meet Drew!

Judging by his formal appearance he had recently stepped off a plane, but why was he here? Had he followed her, or had he arrived purely by chance? Did he intend to squeeze mercilessly at her bruised heart by revealing that he and Tamsin were a twosome again or—her breath halted—had he tracked down further unpaid bills he could attribute to Charlie, and thus to her? His rapid strides up through the tables shook her out of her paralysis.

'Come on, poppet,' he smiled, and reached for her hand, pulling her close to kiss her brow, the bristly moustache grazing her skin. Held close in his arms, Nicole was uncomfortably aware of how little she was wearing as the woollen suit met the bare length of her arms and legs.

'Nicki and I became engaged a few days ago,' he announced, steering her down into the dazzle of lights.

The following silence was rent by a sharp intake of breath from Tamsin, but she was a professional and

recovered quickly to set her mouth into a fixed smile
and offer the necessary congratulations.

Surprise made Nicole catch her breath, too, and she
flashed Drew a puzzled glance. So he had no intention
of renewing his affair with the singer! For a moment her
heart spun with giddy joy, but the brief elation faded.
He was emphasising to Tamsin that she was discarded
and for good, yet, at the same time, he was informing
everyone on Key Benedict that Nicole was his fiancée.
The band, supposedly sorting out their music scores,
were listening, and she had no doubt the news would
spread like wildfire. On the island everyone knew Drew,
or knew of him, and now they would know of her. She
gritted her teeth. Originally she had understood their
engagement to be an announcement in a newspaper,
nothing more, but she had reckoned without Drew's
scheme of things. Back in England he had made her
deceive his family, and now on this side of the Atlantic
he seemed intent on spreading the falsehood further.
She snatched her hand from his. He would not make
her lie to José, Rochelle and Jean. They did not deserve
that, and neither did she!

'It's not a real engagement,' she said, as Tamsin
switched instantly on to red alert. If the words were not
the emphatic denial Nicole longed to make they were,
at least, a first lunge for freedom. 'It was one of those
rash impulses,' she continued, shrugging carelessly.
'Seemed like a good idea at the time, but——'

She broke off mid-stream as Drew's fingers bit into
the tender flesh of her upper arm.

'But now an engagement is unnecessary,' he
continued, smoothly taking over the narrative.

Nicole glanced up at him with a spurt of unexpected
hope at his words. Idly he stretched a long finger
beneath her chin, tipping her head until she was
drowning in the depths of those dangerous blue eyes.
Mist obliterated Tamsin and the musicians. Drew had

captured her as effectively as if he had fastened a ball and chain to each ankle.

'It's unnecessary because we're going to be married next month,' he added, and kissed her full on the mouth.

Her brief hope crashed to the ground. So he had no intention of breaking off their phoney engagement! But what did he want? What devious step came next? She squirmed beneath the drugging sweetness of his lips, fighting for the strength to expose his deceit.

'You must be very much in love,' Tamsin's voice observed, pulling her back into the real world as Drew ended the kiss.

The band crowded around, slapping him on the back and uttering the clichés of congratulation. For years Charlie had drummed good manners into her, and now it was sheer habit which had her smiling and accepting the good wishes, when all the time she burned to shriek that he was a hypocrite. Loathe scenes she might, but everyone has their limits, and Nicole had almost reached hers. If only she had the courage to shock everyone rigid by throwing a tantrum and revealing Drew for the monster he was! But good manners and social cowardice kept her silent as they took their leave.

'This way,' Drew ordered when he saw she was about to explode, and he marched her into the lift, only waiting until the doors slid together before he hauled her into his arms.

'Let me go! Leave me alone!'

He paid no attention, instead holding her close and grabbing kisses where he could as she thrashed around in his arms. The lift moved upwards, but Nicole was hardly aware of the motion. Now she was intent on fighting for her physical freedom, red-hot anger filling her brain as she twisted against him, conscious of the unrelenting firmness of his muscles beneath the formal suit. The fact that he appeared to be holding her without any effort at all added fuel to her anger. Oh, he was so big, so all-powerful—so aroused . . .

Quite unexpectedly she realised that by wriggling in his arms she was making both their temperatures rise. Drew had an arm around her waist and had slipped his hand beneath her skimpy top to splay firm fingers across her back. There was a darkening of desire in the blue eyes that smiled down so patronisingly at her feverish attempts to escape. Nicole stood quite still. There was a pause and then she started up again, this time with words. A torrent of accusations poured from her lips, insults bouncing off the lift walls and turning the air blue.

'That's one hell of a vocabulary you've got there,' Drew grinned when she paused for breath. 'Did they teach you that in Switzerland?'

'Damn Switzerland,' she stormed. 'And damn you!'

'Me?' Cocking his head to one side, Drew adopted a martyred air. 'Don't tell me my halo's crooked?'

'Crooked!'

Nicole was lost for words. She was still searching for choice expressions with which to tell him exactly what she thought of his scheming, when the lift stopped and the doors slid apart. Breathing heavily, she yanked herself free and stalked into the corridor, not caring which floor they were on, or where she was heading. Drew grabbed hold of her shoulder and guided her forward, his fingers tightening to keep her quiet as they paused to allow a couple of hotel guests to pass.

'In here,' he said when they rounded a corner.

He unlocked a door, pushing it wide to reveal the luxury of a standard hotel apartment.

'No show villa this time?' she taunted, her face flushed with anger.

Nicole stood back, feet set firmly apart, refusing to follow the wave of his hand and go in before him. From now on she would control her own life. Drew Benedict could go to hell! He shrugged, though whether it was at the jibe or her refusal to enter the room, she could not decide. Walking ahead, Drew swivelled and ran a hand through his dark hair.

'Come on in,' he smiled. A spider beckoning to a fly could not have been pleasanter—nor as treacherous. 'We have things to say.'

'Nice try, but no,' snapped Nicole, well aware she could not afford to trust either of them. Her pulse rate had not yet steadied from his kisses in the lift and she had a shrewd suspicion Drew was also breathing a little too heavily.

'Don't you want to hear what I discoverd in Tenerife?' he asked, strolling off into the living-room.

Nicole glowered at his retreating shoulders. 'No.'

'It makes good listening,' he threw back.

Aware he was sapping her resistance, she clung to the doorframe. 'Tell me out here.'

A group of laughing children in swimming gear ran along the corridor, and Drew waited until they had passed before replying.

'I refuse to discuss anything with every Tom, Dick and Harry listening in,' he retorted, jamming his lips stubbornly together.

Halfheartedly she straightened, unable to persuade herself to make a clean break and march away. 'Did you know I was here on Key Benedict?'

'Naturally. I rang the apartment a couple of times and there was no reply. I realised something was afoot the minute I questioned Brian. He couldn't lie his way out of a paper bag!'

'Not like his brother!'

The blue eyes sparkled. 'Hugo or Paul?'

His air of benign affability prodded Nicole into a further scathing description of his personality defects. Bloodied but unbowed, Drew grinned at her.

'Hush,' he said, raising a finger to his lips. 'You'll

frighten the other guests. Come in and I'll tell you all I've discovered about your beloved Charlie—and Roberto.'

The yellow lights in her eyes flashed.

'My word, you really pried into my past, didn't you?' she snarled, a wave of pure fury breaking over her. How dared he poke and pry like this! Now such minor considerations as being in or out of his room were inconsequential and she strode forward, hands on hips, quivering with rage. 'Well, I hope you're satisfied! Did it give you a vicarious thrill to discover Roberto left me because he needed a wealthier woman?' It hardly registered that Drew had closed the door behind her. 'Ironical, isn't it?' she demanded. 'Finance always seems to be a problem between me and men. Roberto was a gigolo, though I was too naïve to realise it at the time. I was foolish enough to imagine he loved me, not Charlie's wealth.'

An emotion suspiciously like pain paled Drew's features. 'Nicki,' he implored, holding out his arms to her.

She took a hesitant step forward, throbbing with the need to go into them, to allow Drew to hold her close and comfort her. But she stopped dead. No matter how painful, it was imperative she purge herself of the past. Shaking her head, she hooked her hands over the back of a velvet wing chair, needing its support.

'For a while I thought Roberto was the love of my life,' she told him. 'In reality it was no more than a holiday romance which required idyllic surroundings and golden days in order to survive. Set Roberto down in the London drizzle and I would have seen through his winning smile within minutes, but——' she lifted and dropped a tapering hand. 'Charlie wasn't too keen on him, but as time went by I think I convinced even him of Roberto's sincerity.' She shook her head in wry bewilderment. 'How mistaken I was!'

Flexing his shoulders, Drew tugged free the buttons of his jacket. 'That was Charlie's big mistake too. He trusted your judgment to the extent of asking the Spaniard to settle all his outstanding accounts.'

Nicole's heart leapt. 'What do you mean?'

'Charles Werner handed over an uncrossed cheque for something like four thousand pounds to Roberto on the day you and he left Tenerife. The Spaniard exchanged it for cash and days later he, too, abandoned the island. It appears he installed himself in some swanky hotel in Marbella with a brand-new wardrobe and a come-hither look angled at middle-aged ladies.'

She swayed against the chair, her head spinning. 'How do you know all this?' she asked weakly.

'You were so convinced of Werner's innocence that I believed you, so I went to Tenerife to get to the heart of the matter. I talked with our man there, and the guy who had been in St Lucia, and they both reckoned not paying his bills had been totally out of character for Charles Werner. They couldn't understand why it had happened.' Drew threw his jacket aside, pausing to roll up his shirtsleeves. 'In conversation it emerged that our man remembered your connection with Roberto. He said that before the Spaniard left he had told everyone that he'd won a lottery. He threw a large party, bought masses of gifts for his family and friends, and then vanished.' Drew slumped a broad shoulder against the window wall. 'We put two and two together, and decided to visit Roberto's family. His mother nearly passed out when we arrived on the doorstep and I said my name was Benedict. Within minutes she was blabbering about a cheque her son had sent to her weeks ago. He wanted her to bank it and send cheques to all the companies on an enclosed list. She showed us the list. It was in English and was not, she reckoned, in Roberto's handwriting, so I imagine Charlie must have provided it, together with the original cheque.'

Slowly Nicole circumnavigated the chair. 'Roberto was repaying the money?'

'Yes, but his mother had realised something was fishy and hesitated. The poor woman was terrified she might wind up in gaol.' Drew stared bleakly out at the sand-dunes. 'Roberto has a—a friend who treats him very generously, I'll leave you to fill in the details yourself.'

'And what happened to the cheque?'

'When we explained how we'd already cleared the other debts she handed it over, she was delighted to be free of it. When the cheque was paid into the bank it was cleared without any trouble.'

Nicole was treading bottomless water. 'So I don't owe you any money?'

'No.'

She frowned. It was taking a few moments for the facts to filter through. 'I'm out of your debt and the phoney engagement can end right now?'

Drew nodded.

Where was ecstatic relief at the knowledge that she was free? Nicole waited, but nothing happened. She knew that pleasure should have greeted her regained independence, but instead there was an odd feeling of— loss? She bit into her lip.

'Did you discover why Charlie travelled all the time?'

The muscled shoulders rose and fell beneath the sky-blue silk of his shirt. 'No. It sounds as though it must have been your mother's activities that dictated the pace when she was alive.' Drew flashed her a glance from beneath his dark curly lashes. 'The man from St Lucia was full of highly spiced stories, though I got the impression he fancied her himself. She must have been quite a fireball! He also said how sorry he felt for you and Werner. You were respectable, wanting to lead decent lives, whereas she——' He turned back to the window, gazing at the waves breaking on the white-sand shore.

'It wasn't easy living with her,' Nicole admitted, then she raised her chin. 'But she was my mother and she wasn't all bad.'

'One thing's in her favour, she had a beautiful daughter,' said Drew. 'You might have inherited her sex appeal, but you haven't inherited her——'

'Waywardness?' Nicole provided.

'Yep.'

'You don't think I'm tainted?' she asked cautiously.

'Good heavens, no! I'd be proud to—to—' he changed his mind about what he was going to say and turned again to the window.

Nicole smiled at his broad back, smothering an urge to clasp her arms around him and kiss the nape of his neck where the dark hair curled over his collar.

'Probably Werner was too old to settle after your mother died,' he continued, switching back to the main thread of the conversation. 'Twenty years on the move would be a difficult habit to break. As far as the financial side is concerned, well——' Drew made a vague gesture, 'commodities can pull the rug from under your feet, but the St Lucia man reckoned that if Werner had had money troubles he was astute enough to make sure no one suffered.'

'So perhaps he did come a cropper?' Nicole mused. As she remembered Charlie's birthday gift, her stomach twisted. 'Do you think I might have acted illegally by accepting money from him and buying the cottage?'

'Don't worry. I'll ask our accountants to look into the matter, and if there's any tax to pay I'll settle it. It seems the least I can do after subjecting you to all my accusations.'

Nicole digested this. 'Brian told me Charlie's debt wasn't too disastrous for the company,' she jibed, with a flare of temper. 'Why did you create such a fuss and make me responsible?'

A seagull landed on the balcony wall and Drew

treated it to a glare of such cold distaste that it flew off again.

'Isn't it obvious? I had to keep you around until I decided what I wanted to do with you.'

Nicole did not know whether to feel pleased or dismayed. 'Wasn't that rather high-handed?'

'Yes, but you knocked me for six and I didn't much like the feeling,' he grated, now tugging at his tie with both hands as though it was a python and he needed to strangle it in order to survive. 'Until then I'd run my life *my* way—no commitments.'

'Why?'

He swore violently. 'Okay, I have this—this hang-up,' he growled. 'On the career side I've been successful— flourishing company, solid assets, healthy bank account, but where it really matters I've failed.'

'You mean your divorce?'

'Yes!' he had mastered the tie, and cast it from him.

'But that was ages ago!'

'I know,' he said, weary now. 'And I know I'm a different man from the boy who got married in the expectation that it would change him into an adult overnight, but——' He gave an indeterminate shrug. It was obvious his revelations were causing him pain.

'But what?' she probed.

'But the divorce really shook me up.' He raised two hands as a buffer. 'I know, I know, divorce is commonplace. It's not the end of the world, most people marry again and are very happy, but when it happens to you, it's different. I suppose I felt guilty because, deep down, I'd gone into marriage for all the wrong reasons, so it was my fault that it failed.'

Nicole tilted her head to one side. 'Why did you get married?'

'In those days I was desperate to shake off the pretty boy image. Already I'd made a success with the houses, raised some cash. I was arrogant enough to believe I was a responsible businessman, a man of the world, and I expected to be regarded as such. At twenty!' He shook his head at his own ignorance. 'All too soon I realised everyone was still mentally patting me on the head, so I decided to impress everyone by getting married. Nothing changed—I was still the boy wonder!'

'And what about your wife?'

He gave a long-drawn-out sigh. 'Karen was as immature as I was. She loved the wedding, and for a while she loved playing at being a housewife, but she became bored. She wanted to go dancing, dine out, impress her friends with holidays abroad. Any spare time I had, I preferred to spend on swotting up company law and such, so conflict set in. When I enrolled for a three-year evening course in accountancy, that brought matters to a head.'

'So you broke up?' she asked.

'Yep. Once everything was final I concluded that marriage was not for me, and I made damn sure I didn't become involved with any woman likely to lead me that way. I don't think it was a conscious decision, it just happened. I embarked on a series of discreet friendships, but they were always secondary to work. I developed into a workaholic to eliminate any suspicion I could be missing out.' His mouth lifted into self-mockery. 'It wasn't easy—what with my mother extolling family life every five minutes! In consequence I ended up flying too much, smoking too much, I was so damned uptight I must have been hell to know.'

'You were—you are,' Nicole inserted ruthlessly.

Drew refused to rise to the bait. 'Okay, I accept that I'm a louse, but don't forget that for the past fourteen years or so I've been convincing myself that I function better alone, and then you arrive to complicate matters.'

'*Me* complicate matters!' she retorted. 'That's rich!'

'First you ignored me, then you tantalised me with

the promise of your spectacular suntan,' he teased, recovering his natural self-confidence now that the painful past had been discarded. 'You seduced me at the villa, and——'

'Not true!' she flared, annoyed at the way Drew had adroitly switched the conversation. 'In any case, our relationship is all finished now.'

He arched a thick brow. 'Is it?'

'*Yes!*' Nicole was not about to make things easy for him. If anyone had to commit themselves, it must be Drew. 'You really are a swine,' she continued, flicking back the glossy hair from her shoulders. 'You knew Charlie's debt had been paid and yet only ten minutes ago you told Tamsin Jay that we were going to be married.'

'I wanted to get her off my back.'

That was not quite the answer Nicole was hoping to hear, and her tone sharpened. 'Well, she's off now and so am I! I'm having nothing more to do with you.'

'If you believe that, you'll believe anything,' said Drew, and swung to inspect the seashore once again.

'And what does that mean?' she demanded, for they seemed to be getting nowhere fast.

'Don't you know how I feel about you?' he mumbled, staring at the sea.

'No!' The word was an icicle, sharp and cold.

Spreading his hands, he turned to her. 'For heaven's sake, darling, you know how it was when we made love. Couldn't you tell then?'

'Tell what?' Nicole was trying to breathe normally.

With the frenzied air of a lemming about to leap over a cliff, Drew said loudly, 'That I love you, dammit!' He ran long fingers through his hair, tumbling the strands all over the place. 'What do you want—blood? I'm out of practice at this kind of thing. I have a mental block as far as commitment is concerned.'

She tried hard to ignore the firecrackers of joy which

were exploding in her brain. 'Bad luck,' she said flippantly.

Drew swallowed hard. 'Okay, I love you, I love you, *I love you*!'

'There's no need to shout!'

Shaking his head in despair, he sank down on to the wing chair. 'Is that all you can say?'

'I'm waiting until you finish.' Nicole gave a devastating smile. 'Have you finished?' Something akin to ecstasy was chasing through her veins.

'No,' he moaned, and sank his head into his hands. 'Oh damn, I'm getting bogged down with all this! You wouldn't settle for a few euphemisms, would you?'

'Like what?' she teased.

He held out his arms and she walked towards him. 'Like you and me living happily forever after?' he asked, pulling her on to his knee.

'I don't know what you mean,' she murmured.

Drew rubbed his hand across her bare thigh. 'Don't be obtuse. You know damn well what I mean. Let's make the engagement real and——' He paused.

'And what?'

With a groan of frustration, Drew buried his head in her shoulder. 'You realise I vowed never to say this again, don't you?'

The suspense was delicious.

The grey-green eyes stretched wide with innocence.

'Say what?'

'I'm going cold all over,' he complained.

'It's Florida fever.'

'Like hell! It's terror.' His head jerked up, the blue eyes ramming into hers. 'You're not going to say no, are you?' he demanded, aghast. 'Oh, Nicki darling, don't say no. I can't live without you. I love you, I want you, we belong together.' His words were tumbling out.

'Say no to what?' she asked calmly.

He rubbed his moustache with the back of his hand. 'To my proposal.'

Slowly Nicole revolved one ankle. 'Is that what this is? And what are you proposing?'

'Marriage,' he groaned. 'Darling, please will you marry me?'

The revolving ankle halted. 'Aren't you supposed to go down on one knee?' she prevaricated, enjoying every minute.

'You really want your pound of flesh, don't you?' groaned Drew, half joking, half exasperated, and made as if to push her from him.

'Don't bother,' Nicole murmured, sliding her arms around his neck. 'Yes, I'll marry you, but only to please your family. They're honest and open, whereas you——'

She felt him chuckle.

'Don't be too harsh,' he pleaded, kissing the smooth skin of her throat. 'I know I've handled everything poorly between us, but—but I'm a little rusty where love is concerned. I don't know how to cope with it. For ages I wavered between patronising you and sweeping you off your feet. I didn't know what to think when the connection with Werner came to light. In one way I suppose I was grateful because it seemed to mean you were flawed, and so, thank goodness, I couldn't love you. At least, not love you enough to marry you. The trouble was that it was obvious you knew nothing about the debts and, in any case, I wanted you so damn much I wouldn't have cared if you'd masterminded the Great Train Robbery.'

Nicole's heart was singing. 'And then you decided I had had an illicit affair with Charlie. You should have seen him, Drew! He was barely five foot five, going bald and as straight-laced as a Presbyterian minister!'

Drew allowed himself a wry smile. 'I never really believed you'd had that kind of relationship with him, but by then I was in such a state of panic I was flinging everything I could lay my hands on. Somehow I had to make you—blemished!'

'It would have been far simpler just to shunt me out of your life,' she smiled.

'I know, but as much as I was terrified of loving you, I was equally terrified you might not love me. The only reason I concocted the idea of us getting engaged was in the hope it might turn out to be what we both wanted.'

'And it has,' she whispered against his lips.

The kiss was long and sweet and total. When Drew released her, Nicole was incapable of sensible thought, and when he said, 'I have something for you,' and reached for his jacket, she clung giddily to him.

Drew fished a small maroon velvet box from his jacket. 'I've been carrying this around for ages, trying to pluck up the courage to give it to you.' He handed it to her. 'For my love,' he said gently.

She raised the lid. Brilliants sparkled in the depths of the diamond solitaire that nestled against the satin. 'It's beautiful,' she said reverently.

The furrow at the side of his mouth lurched. 'It's passé to make love wearing a single diamond, now you'll be at the height of fashion in two. Hurry up and put it on.' His blue eyes gleamed. 'You could be right about me having another dose of that Florida fever. I can feel my temperature beginning to rise, and if I'm afflicted, chances are you could be, too!'

Nicole nodded gravely. 'What shall we do?'

'Doctor's orders would be to go to bed until the crisis passes.'

She slipped the ring on her finger. 'And how long do you think the crisis is going to last?'

'A lifetime,' Drew murmured, and bent his head to kiss her.

A WORD ABOUT THE AUTHOR

Although her first novel wasn't penned until she was nearly forty, Elizabeth Oldfield actually began writing professionally when she was a teenager. She had enrolled in a writing course taught by mail. As guaranteed, the course more than paid for itself with money she subsequently earned from sales of her writing to magazines and newspapers—but at that stage of her life, writing was really only a hobby. Soon other types of work outside the home and family life took her away from dreams of living by her pen.

After a number of years of marriage, her husband, a mining engineer, was posted to Singapore for a five-year spell. Here Elizabeth enjoyed not only exciting leisure activities—tennis, handicrafts, entertaining fascinating visitors from all over the globe—but also the opportunity to absorb as much as possible about a culture as varied as it was exotic. And having more time on her hands, she resumed her writing—once again finding success at articles, interviews and humorous pieces.

But she had a larger goal: to write a book. Romance novels caught her eye. By the time she left Singapore, she had completed two novels and eventually saw both published—sending her on her way as a romance novelist. Now she works four days a week on her books, spending the rest of her time in various activities, including, whenever possible, hours spent with her family.